Why Should I Love You? 3

Ivy Symone

Acknowledgments

First and foremost, I must acknowledge and give a major shout out to all of my readers! Without you guys, I wouldn't be so driven. I appreciate all of the love and support you guys have shown.

And of course, I'd like to thank my mother Brenda Lockett, my cousin Geneva Mitchell, daughter India Bradford, and my sister Ebony Woods for being encouraging. Love you guys! Oh, and hey to my little ones Harrah, AJ, and Dion! Love you!

Chapter 1

Something didn't feel right. The premonition was so profound; it was enough to wake Eli from his slumber.

Sitting up in bed, he looked out into the darkness of his bedroom. He was only able to make out certain things from the moon's illuminating glow peering through his windows. *What's wrong with you*, he asked himself. He was bugging.

Lying back down, he closed his eyes as soon as his head hit the pillow. Again, the feeling came back. His eyes opened, but he didn't move. He listened. Something or someone was in his house.

Eli's first thought was to grab his cellphone from the nightstand. He quickly found Abe's name in his recent calls and hit the call button; after three rings, Abe answered in an irritated, groggy tone.

"What?"

Eli whispered, "Abe!"

"What nigga! Why the fuck you calling me—"

"Abe! There's someone in my house!"

There was silence.

"Abe?" Eli queried. "Did you hear—"

"Yeah, I heard you!" Abe irately said.

Lovely's voice could be heard in the background as she asked, "What is it, Abe?"

Eli asked, "What should I do?"

"Why are you calling me? Nigga, call nine one-one!"

There was the rhythmic sound of feet running. Eli's heart thumped in his chest wildly. "Abe! It's more than one of them!"

With a little more concern, Abe finally said, "Eli, hit the damn panic button on your security system, call the damn police, and I'll be over there."

Lovely asked, "What's going on, Abe?"

Abe explained to Lovely that Eli thought someone was in his house. Lovely laughed, "Uhm, he do have kids now. Maybe it's them."

Abe sighed, "Eli? Go check on the kids."

"Like hell I am!" Eli exclaimed. "I'm staying right here. They gon' have to fend for themselves."

"Eli! What kind of father are you?" Abe asked with aggravation.

"Not a good one," Eli replied. "They can get got!"

"Eli, take your ass in there and see—"

"Ssh!" Eli hushed him quietly. The sound of the feet got closer to his bedroom. *Oh shit*, he thought. He whispered in the phone, "This'll be the last time I talk to you Abe. I love you. I'm about to die."

Abe started laughing.

"This shit ain't funny!"

"Yes, it is," Abe laughed.

"Ssh!"

Eli became very still as he listened. His door opened wider. They were whispering. He could imagine his intruders whispering about who was going to do what.

"Eli?" Abe called.

Eli ignored his brother. He closed his eyes and recited the Lord's Prayer in his head. As soon as he felt the hand on him, he screamed and jumped at the same time, causing his intruders to scream too.

Bria was startled so bad she started crying. Eli quickly switched on the lamp on his nightstand.

Bryce gave Eli the angry eyes. "Why you scare us like that?"

Eli sighed with relief. "Oh hell, it's just the kids."

"Eli, I'ma kick your ass!" Abe threatened.

"C'mere Bria," Eli said reaching out for her sympathetically. "I'm sorry, but y'all scared the shit out of me."

"Why you so scary, Eli?" Bryce asked. His tone was mocking.

"I'm not scary," Eli pulled Bria into the bed and hugged her to him. "As a matter of fact, I was trying to calm your Uncle Abe down. He was worried and was about to come over here. I told him I had the situation under control."

"You hear this shit?" Abe asked no one in particular.

Lovely said, "We need to go get those kids and let them just stay here."

"Okay Abe," Eli said into the phone. "I got this. No worries here. But thanks anyway."

"Are you sure?" Abe asked.

"Yeah...," Eli was hesitant. He covered his mouth and whispered into the phone, "Can you just come by and check the perimeters out?"

"I'm going back to bed," Abe said before hanging up.

"Mothafucka," Eli said under his breath. He looked at his two children looking back at him. He asked, "Why are y'all not asleep?"

Bria looked up at Eli with her eyes still glistening with the tears. "We miss our mama."

Eli was stuck. Usually, when the twins had these moments, another adult such as Lovely or Aunt Livy was around to comfort and console the twins. Eli wasn't good at things like that. He tried to think of something comforting to say.

"Well... I know. Hey, how about we go find something to snack on?"

"Mama didn't let us eat junk food at night," Bryce said.

"Well, your mama ain't here," Eli said. He realized how insensitive it was as soon as it left his lips. Bria started whimpering again. He tried to fix it. "I'm sorry. But you're with me now. And I say it's okay to eat junk food at night."

"Eating junk food at night will give us bad dreams," Bria whined.

"And who told you that?" Eli asked.

"That's what Granny and Mama told us," Bryce said.

"That's some bullshit," Eli dismissed.

"You're cursing," Bria reminded Eli.

"Oops," Eli said. He smiled at them with guilt and shame. "I'm sorry. I'm supposed to be watching that, huh?"

Bria finally cracked a smile as she nodded. Eli couldn't help but adore how pretty she was. It was one thing when he thought the twins could possibly be his; but now that he knew they were his, they were definitely finding their own special place in his heart.

"Hold on," Eli said. He grabbed his phone and dialed Abe again.

Abe answered in a more sluggish tone. "What?"

"Ask Lovely if kids are like Gremlins. Will they turn if I feed them at night?"

Lovely smiled to herself. She could feel Abe behind her, trying to get comfortable again. He was restless and couldn't find the right position to lie in. Eli's call threw Abe off. He let out a deep, long breath that expressed how irritated he truly was.

"Abe?" Lovely queried without turning around.

Abe blurted, "Why did he do that shit!"

Lovely giggled. "That's your brother."

"Something is seriously wrong with Eli. I think Mama dropped him more than once on his head when he was a baby," Abe quipped.

"Perhaps..." Lovely chuckled.

Silence fell between them. Lovely's mind was all over the place. One thought couldn't finish developing without another one invading. There was the foundation she and Abe were working on. All of the chairs on the board needed to be filled. Then there was the planning of this extravagant wedding Abe wanted to have by their anniversary. Lovely wasn't sure if she really wanted a wedding. Being pregnant again; she was sure her belly would be noticeable. That was the reason she was against a wedding the first time they married.

Lovely's mind drifted to the recent death of Kiera, the twins' mother. It was a shame she had to leave this world so soon. Lovely had grown fond of her in the past few months. While Lovely could admit she had been leery of the girl at first, she quickly discovered Kiera wasn't so bad after all. She just needed to surround herself with more positive people in her life. The good in her had begun to come out, but her life ended so tragically. It left Eli a newly single father of two, instantly. He was still adapting. So far, he hadn't been too bad. It had only been a few days. Lovely figured a couple of months from now, Eli would be a pro at being a parent.

The past also found its way into Lovely's mind. She wondered where her uncle Mano was in the investigation of her parents' death. She wanted to know if he had any leads of where these people were; the home invaders that changed her life drastically. She knew Abe didn't approve of her looking into it, but he had to understand that this was something she needed.

Abe tapped Lovely on the shoulder, "Baby?"

"Hmm?"

"You sleep?"

"Yep," Lovely answered with a giggle.

"Can I tell you something?"

"I'm sleep though."

He rolled over on his side to face Lovely's exposed back. The skylight overhead cast enough of a glow for him to see the feminine contours of her shoulders and neck; there was something very delicate and graceful about Lovely, even as she laid there. She was like an exquisite piece of art that no matter how bold the letters warning *not to touch* were; Abe just had to touch her. He had to explore her body every time she was near.

"Lovely," Abe whispered. He kissed her shoulder softly. His hand cupped her breast and began to massage it gently. Her nipple grew rigid, immediately, pressing against the soft material of her slip gown. A moan escaped her lips. Abe pressed his body into hers, making her aware of his urgent desire for her.

"*Te amo mi amor*," he whispered in her ear as he nibbled on her lobe.

Lovely turned to face him. With the room being dark, she could barely make him out, but somehow, she always knew where his lips were. She kissed him fervently before slowly easing a trail of kisses down his neck. She gently pushed him, so he would lie on his back.

"What are you doing?" Abe whispered as Lovely straddled him.

Lovely put her finger up to her lips to silence him. She brought her mouth down to his bare skin and kissed his chest. She found his nipples and encircled them with the soft strokes of her tongue. Moving further down, she placed kisses down his chest and over his abdomen. As her body brushed against his, Lovely could feel the hardness of Abe growing beneath her.

Abe stopped Lovely when she reached the waistband of his boxer briefs. He asked again, “What are you doing?”

“Trying to please my man,” Lovely responded. She went for his waistband again.

Abe grabbed her hand. “You don’t have to.”

Lovely shook his hand from hers. “Let me.”

Abe watched Lovely free his dick, wrapping her dainty hands around it. She looked so cute and sexy at the same time as her loose, curly, hair hung in her face. A smile crept across Abe’s face as he adored his wife’s efforts.

Lovely took in an anxious breath and slowly exhaled it, preparing herself for this challenge. Just the thought of putting a penis in her mouth made her gag reflexes act up. She heaved one time and heard Abe snickering. She heaved again.

“Didn’t I tell you, you didn’t have to do it?” Abe fussed.

Annoyed by the amusement in his voice, Lovely released him from her grasp and crawled back to her side of the bed. She turned her back to him.

“Lovely, what’s wrong?” Abe asked softly. He moved close behind her once more and wrapped his arm around her.

Lovely pouted, “I wanna satisfy you orally, but I can’t do it.”

“And I told you not to worry about that. How many times I gotta tell you?”

“I know. It’s just that...” her voice trailed. She sighed. “What man doesn’t want head from his woman?”

“I... uhm... it’s not really,” he cleared his throat, “...necessary.”

Lovely groaned. "Yeah, it is. You want your dick sucked!"

"I didn't say that."

"You might as well. What good am I if I can't give you head?" She turned on her back.

"Giving head doesn't determine—"

Lovely interrupted him by asking, "Did Aisha and Kenya suck your dick?"

Abe hesitantly said, "They did."

"See!"

"But it—"

"And I bet they did it well too."

This was awkward, Abe thought. He cleared his throat while trying to clear memories of his ex-girlfriends' superb fellatio skills, and carefully replied. "You know what? How about—"

"They were. Do you miss getting head, Abe?" Lovely asked.

"No," he answered. He brushed the hair wildly covering the side of her face back. He caressed her face with the back of his hand in a loving way. He said softly, "You don't need to do that to please me. Your efforts alone are a turn on to me."

Lovely didn't respond. She enjoyed the sensation of his rock-hard dick poking her in the thigh. She smiled.

Abe asked in an alluring tone. "You know what you can do for me?" Not giving her the opportunity to answer him, he rolled to his back pulling her on top of him. "C'mon and ride this dick."

Lovely giggled. Maybe she couldn't get her gag reflexes in check to suck dick, but she sure knew how to ride one.

Chapter 2

Eli wasn't used to his house being so noisy. He had to ask himself, *why did I agree to this?* He had everybody's children at his house. He was sure his white on white living room would be ruined by the time they left. He was regretting that decision now. There were spills in the kitchen, fingerprints on the walls and windows, Cheetos on his rug in the family room; and Eli was exasperated. He needed Lulu in his house for times like this.

Kenya showed up first to get her kids. *Thank God,* Eli thought. They were the worst.

"You alright?" Kenya asked with a humored smile.

"Yeah, it's just it's too many kids in my house," Eli said. He watched Bria place a beaded necklace she made around Kenya's daughter's neck.

"They get along pretty good, huh?" Kenya asked eyeing the two girls.

Eli nodded. Trying to be a good parent and allowing Lovely to persuade him, Eli agreed to let the twins have a sleepover. He wanted to do all he could to keep their minds off of the loss of their mother.

The front door opened and in walked Robin. She was wearing a smile until her eyes landed on Kenya. Robin cut her eyes at her. She looked past her and smiled at Eli, "I'm here to help, baby."

"Half of 'em upstairs and the other half are downstairs," Eli mumbled.

Robin placed her hand lightly on Eli's chest and asked sincerely, "Are you okay?"

"I'm fine. You know how I get. It's these kids," Eli smiled. Robin returned the smile and let her hand graze his chest as he walked away. Eli didn't know why Robin had touched him so intimately. *Was she trying to prove a point to Kenya?*

"That girl is a trip," Kenya scoffed. She shook her head remembering some of the things Kiera mentioned about Robin. She called out, "C'mon you two. Kev, Kayla!"

Good, Eli thought. *Two down, five to go*. Well, three to go; Bria and Bryce lived there.

After Kenya left, Eli found Robin in the kitchen, cleaning up behind the kids. Robin asked, "Who all is here?"

"Eric's two, Grace, Bria, and Bryce," Eli answered.

"All those big ass kids can't clean up after themselves?" Robin asked.

"Well, I kinda got them spoiled," Eli said sheepishly.

Robin shook her head and laughed as Eli's cell phone rang.

He answered. "Hello?"

Seconds later, Kris said, "Hello?"

Eli was thrown. This was a very pleasant surprise.

"Hey," he said. He shot a quick glance Robin's way.

"What's up?" Kris asked in her soft voice.

Eli turned his back to Robin. “Are you still here?”

“No. But I was calling to let you know I would be back in a few weeks.”

“Oh.” All kind of thoughts began running through Eli’s head.

“You think we could hook up when I get there?”

“Sure,” Eli answered quickly.

Kris giggled lightly. “We have some unfinished business to discuss.”

“Yeah, we do. You never had a chance to tell me what it was you had to tell me.”

“Right; so, I’ll call you when I touch down.”

“That sounds good,” Eli said. The thought of seeing Kris again put a smile on his face.

“Well, I gotta go. I’ll talk to you later. And Eli, take care of yourself. I love you.”

Eli wanted to reciprocate the words but found it difficult to get them out.

Kris laughed again. “You don’t have to say anything Eli. Just take care, okay?”

“Okay. Bye,” he said ending the call. When he spun around, Robin was staring a hole in him.

“Who was that?”

There was no reason to lie. He owed Robin nothing. Shit, he wasn’t her man.

“That was my friend.”

“What friend?”

"It was my friend, Kris."

Robin stood there, trying to recall where she had heard that name before. Then it clicked. She chuckled, "That thing from the party?"

Eli shot Robin a daggered look.

Ignoring Eli's stare, Robin asked, "So what does she want?"

"Not that it's any of your business, but she just wanna come through and talk to me."

"And she couldn't say what she needed to say just then?"

Eli shook his head disapprovingly. "No, Robin. Don't start that."

"So, she's coming over here now?"

"Why?" Eli asked out of aggravation.

Robin rested a hand on her hip and shifted her weight to one side. Narrowing her eyes at Eli suspiciously, she asked, "Do you and her have something going on?"

"Robin!" Eli exclaimed with frustration.

Eli's tone didn't faze Robin. "So, since when did you like fucking women that look like little boys?"

"Who said anything about fucking? Is that all you think about? Why is it that I can't have a simple friendship with someone else without the thought of sex, Robin?"

"Cause I know you... And I've noticed how you get all sensitive and defensive when it comes to that girl."

"If I did, it would be my personal business. I don't have to share that with you. And for your information, I find Kris very attractive. She's different. She's her own person."

"So, do you have something going on with her?"

Eli let out an exasperated sigh. "What if I did?"

Robin's expression changed to one of hurt and disappointment. "What about me?"

"What about you?"

"You're not interested in me anymore, but you want to be with a woman that clearly looks like a sixteen-year-old boy!"

"She does not," Eli argued.

Robin's anger grew. She taunted, "So you might be gay after all."

"There you go with that same shit."

"Am I not good enough anymore? Do I need to go buy a dick and chop my titties off?" Robin asked sarcastically.

"Dad?"

Eli swung around and saw Bryce standing in the entryway of the kitchen. Grace was with him. They looked stunned which told Eli they heard Robin.

Bryce looked at Robin, then at his father. "Uhm...I just wanted the Cheetos."

"Okay. Please don't drop them everywhere," Eli said. He gestured to Robin to walk toward the back toward the home office. Once inside, Eli asked, "What is wrong with you?"

"Shit, they ain't little kids that don't know nothing. What does it matter?"

"They may know, but they don't need to hear things like you chopping your titties off and buying dicks!" Eli scolded. "Sit down and stop being a big ass baby."

"I'm not being a baby. You're hurting me with this gay shit," Robin said angrily. She sat on the sofa.

"You really need to shut the fuck up," Eli snapped. Although Robin was there bitching in his face, Eli still couldn't help thinking of Kris. Time couldn't move fast enough so that he could be graced by her presence again.

As Kenya headed to her driver's side door to get in her car, the sight of a very familiar expensive luxury sports car caught her attention. She stood there, eyeing the vehicle as it pulled up beside hers under Eli's portico. Her lips widened into a smile as she watched Abe get out of the car. *Such a beautiful man*, she thought.

"Hey, Abe!"

Abe cut his eyes at her as he turned to go towards Eli's front entrance.

"You're not gonna speak?" Kenya asked stepping away from her car.

"I ain't got shit to say to you."

"Wait," she said catching him before he could reach for the door. "We don't have to be like this with each other."

"We don't?" Abe asked with skepticism.

Kenya shook her head. "We can still be cordial in all of this."

"What's all of this?"

"You know, your little secret."

Abe diverted his gaze to her car, noticing her kids in the backseat. He lowered his voice and asked, “What the fuck did you say to Lovely?”

Kenya smiled innocently, “What are you talking about?”

Abe stared down at her coldly. “You know what the fuck I’m talking about. Don’t play with me Kenya.”

“I have no clue what you’re talking about.”

Abe moved in closer and said through gritted teeth, “Bitch, you know what the fuck I’m talking about. Don’t make me choke your ass out in front of your kids.”

Kenya gasped with fear while taking a step back. “Kiera said you were crazy.”

“You ain’t seen crazy yet. Keep fucking with me,” Abe threatened. “Say another goddamn thing to Lovely and see what the fuck happens.”

Kenya tried not to let her fear show. She felt like she still had the upper hand in all of this. She cleared her throat. “You know Abe, we can squash this if we make a deal.”

Abe shook his head with defeat. *Here she goes*, he thought. He exhaled heavily and asked, “What do you want, how much?”

Kenya shook her head. “I don’t want money.”

“Well, what do you want?”

“How about you come by my place tomorrow, and we can discuss it.”

“Nope, how about I meet you, Monday?”

"But my house is a much better place for this meeting," she said in a conniving tone. She added, "My bedroom to be exact."

Abe cut his eyes at her as he turned away to enter Eli's home. He left her standing there with her dumb ass grin on her face. *Fuck her*, Abe thought. Kevin Jr. and Kayla would be without a mother soon.

Chapter 3

Lorenzo sat back, relaxing in the oversized chair with his feet propped up on the matching ivory ottoman. He sipped on expensive Remy Martin XO cognac out of a thick crystal glass as he gazed out into Nashville's night sky. He could get used to this all over again. It had been a while since he lived this good.

"Hey Unc," Lorenzo called out. Not waiting for a reply, Lorenzo asked, "How much this condo run you?"

Esau walked over to join his nephew in the living room's sitting area, next to the floor to ceiling windows. "Why are you asking about these? I thought after we handle this business you were going to head West as a new you."

"Yeah, but I wouldn't mind having a spot here to come to. You know, when I wanna see Mama and my kids." Lorenzo answered thoughtfully.

Esau took a sip of his drink. "So, how are your kids?"

"They cool," Lorenzo replied.

"You wouldn't want to take them with you?"

"Hell naw. Tenisha, Gina, and—naw I take that back. Tenisha trifling ass probably would let me take Lil' Lo, but Gina and Carrie ain't gon let me take my kids. I'll just break them off real good so they asses won't be on a nigga's nuts all the goddamn time."

"What about your other child?" Esau asked.

The front door opened. It was Robin letting herself in. She looked over at the two men as she made her way directly to the kitchen.

Lorenzo's eyes followed the plumpness of Robin's ass as she moved about in the kitchen. Without taking his eyes from Robin, he asked Esau, "What other child?"

Choosing not to address the lustful stare his nephew was giving his girl, Esau said, "Grace. Don't you want to get to know her?"

Lorenzo turned his attention back to Esau. He let her name escape his lips softly, "Grace."

"Please," Robin said from the kitchen. She walked over to where they were sitting. "You have a better chance of winning the lottery before they let you have anything to do with Grace."

Lorenzo grinned deviously. "See, that's where you're mistaken. With Abe out the picture, Lovely will bow down to me. And Grace will have no choice but to get to know her real daddy."

"What do you mean, Lovely will bow down to you?" Robin asked with confusion. "I thought the plan was to get rid of her too."

"Maybe," Lorenzo answered nonchalantly.

Robin looked at Esau for an answer. Esau shrugged. Robin hated that Esau had gotten Lorenzo involved in their plans, but then again, Lorenzo did all of the grimy things necessary to make the plans go smoothly. However, it gave Lorenzo a sense of power and control. He took that and thought he could rule over them too.

Robin asked Esau, "So, what about that other little problem?"

Esau was about to answer but was interrupted by his phone ringing. Seeing who it was, he started smiling as he answered. "Speak of the devil. Hello? Okay."

Just like that, Esau ended the call. He didn't bother responding to both Robin's and Lorenzo's questioning gazes. He immediately dialed another number and motioned for them to be quiet.

The person on the other end answered. "Hello?"

"Hey son," Esau said in a worried voice. "Have you talked to your mama?"

"Not for a couple of days," Eli replied. "Why?"

"I hadn't heard from her either. I thought she would have at least talked to you."

"Well, Mama isn't one of my favorite people nowadays."

"What about Abe? You think he may have talked to her?"

"Probably not; Mama probably somewhere with Aunt Mary, spending money, did you call Aunt Mary?"

"I haven't. I'll call her next. But if you don't mind son, can you call Abe and check with him. I'm worried. She's never stayed away this long without telling me where she is."

"What do you mean, stay away this long? How long has she been gone?"

"It's been a few days."

"A few days? You haven't talked to her at all?" Eli asked with concern.

"No. That's why I'm calling you."

"Are y'all still arguing about the shit that happened in the past?" Eli wanted to know.

"Well, we haven't really resolved that. I mean, we pretty much decided there's definitely some counseling needed if we're gonna make this marriage work from here on out."

Eli chuckled with amusement, "Really? Esau, you might as well hang that up, Mama don't want you anymore anyway. Hell, you were sleeping with my baby mama."

"Was," Esau corrected. "That was such a long time ago. It was a mistake. I was weak and tempted."

"Mmm hmm," Eli hummed in doubt. "Well, let me call Abe to see if he's heard from Mama."

"Okay. Call me immediately when you find out anything."

"Okay," Eli said before ending the call.

Esau made sure his line was disconnected. He smiled at Robin and looked at Lorenzo. "How was that?"

Robin smiled, "Perfect."

"So, what's up with that bitch wife of yours?" Lorenzo asked.

"Scottie and Tee said it's taken care of," Esau beamed. "That bitch is out of the way; on to the next thing."

Her caramelized bronze skin tone radiated against the soft, coral color of the cap sleeve cashmere tunic she wore. It was perfectly paired with floral-print, skinny-leg pants that grabbed her every curve. She moved with a gracefulness that hinted at no visual impairment whatsoever. Even the way her doe-like eyes gazed into the faces of her loved ones; a person couldn't tell that the only images she could see were blurred outlines.

Cesar watched Lovely as she spoke with Cece and Luciano. Cece was holding the baby, but Lovely stood close by, ensuring that her son was okay in the older woman's arms.

"Lovely, he's getting so big," Cece crooned.

"I know. He eats all day," Lovely said.

Luciano beamed with pride at his daughter-in-law and grandson. "I'm so glad you stopped by. Where's that son of mine?"

"He's somewhere with Eric," Lovely answered.

"He is?" Cesar asked as he stepped further into his father's den.

Lovely turned in his direction and smiled, "Cesar, you're still in town?"

"Yeah," he said as he greeted her with a kiss on the cheek and a hug.

"I thought you would be long gone by now," Lovely said. AJ began whining, and Lovely immediately went into Mommy-rescue mode.

"I'll take him," Lulu reached for the baby. "You enjoy visit."

"I think he's sleepy, Lulu," Lovely said.

Cesar observed Lovely's actions as she interacted with Lulu and the baby. He could tell Lovely took her parenting seriously. She wasn't one for letting a handicap prevent her from being what she needed to be to her kids. She was the same way with Grace when she was younger. That was one of Lovely's strengths that Cesar admired. However, his admiration didn't stop there. Cesar's eyes roamed the soft feminine contours of Lovely's body.

One of Luciano's housekeepers walked into the den. "Sir, you have a Mr. Chapman here to see you."

"I'll be right there," Luciano said. He looked at Lovely, "Don't go anywhere. This should take just a few minutes."

"I'll be right here," Lovely said.

"We'll be right back," Cece said softly as she followed Luciano.

Lovely turned to Cesar, "So, why are you still here? You're usually somewhere overseas."

"Yeah, I'm just relaxing for a little while," he said. He couldn't resist the urge to brush the strands of hair back that were loosely hanging over her face. "So, you're growing your hair again?"

"I figured it was time for a different look," she said. "Abe likes me with shorter hair though."

"You're beautiful either way," Cesar said.

"Yeah, you're supposed to say that," she said playfully. "What's been going on with you?"

"Nothing much, trying to oversee operations of the business."

Lovely smiled slyly, "What about your love life?"

"What love life?" he asked. He smiled at her. "Lovely, why do you always ask me about my love life?"

"Because you've been single your whole life. Everyone needs a special someone in their life at some point."

"I tried to have a special someone in my life, remember?" Cesar watched Lovely carefully to see how she would react.

Just as he suspected, uneasiness settled over her. Her once playful smile faded. She actually stepped away from him.

To put her back at ease, Cesar said. "But there's no need in rehashing the past. Things are what they are. I'm glad you're happy with Abe."

Lovely nodded as her smile began to return, "Yeah. I truly am. You'll be happy with someone one day too, Cesar."

"Maybe," he said. He shortened the space between them to the point it caused Lovely to gasp. In a lowered soft tone, Cesar said, "You're still the most beautiful being God has created."

Unlike before, Lovely didn't take a step back. She kept her eyes lowered feeling somewhat guilty. Cesar was no longer the older man she had a crush on; he was her husband's half-brother now. It didn't feel right remembering old feelings she once had. Furthermore, Lovely resented Cesar for even hinting around at them after they agreed to never speak of what was or could have been.

"I wished you had waited just a little longer," Cesar whispered.

Lovely shook her head. "Don't Ceez. I don't appreciate this one bit."

Cesar tried to grab her arm as she walked away from him. "Wait! I'm sorry. I was out of line."

"You damn right you were," Lovely spoke angrily. She lowered her voice, "Why now? Why would you go there with me now?"

"I don't know. It's just the more I see you in this role of being someone else's wife... I didn't think it would bother me so much. But I hear how Abe talks about you. I see how happy you make him. I want that."

"You can have that."

Cesar grabbed her hand and brought it to his lips. He kissed it softly. "But how can I when you're his wife?"

Lovely jerked her hand back. "You can't have it with me. You can have it with someone else."

"No. Someone else won't do."

Lovely was about to respond, but her phone interrupted her. She pressed her blue tooth device to answer.

"Hey!"

"Where are you?" Abe asked.

Lovely couldn't make out the exact tone of Abe's voice, but it didn't sound normal. "Are you okay?"

"Answer my question," he demanded.

"I'm at Lu's. Why? What's the matter?" Lovely asked with concern.

There was silence, but Lovely could hear a lot of background noise, "Abe? What is it?"

"It's my mama."

"What about her?"

"Look, just stay at Lu's until I come to get you," Abe said. Lovely could hear the weariness in his voice.

"Abe, what's wrong?" Lovely asked.

Ignoring Lovely's question, Abe asked, "Where's AJ?"

"Lulu has him. They're here with me."

"Okay. Y'all just stay put until I come," he said.

"Okay."

"Lovely?"

"Yes?"

"I love you."

"I love you too," she said softly. She expected the usual playfulness as Abe always did on the phone; neither one of them wanting to end the call, but Abe immediately ended the call.

"What was that about?" Cesar asked.

Lovely thought to herself; *something is going on. He didn't sound right. I'm almost afraid to know.*

Something definitely wasn't right. *Could this all be a big coincidence?* First, Kiera's death, and not even a whole week after burying her, another major incident has happened. There was something unnerving about all of this.

As Abe stood by the double picture windows of his mother's hospital room, his mind began to wander. Kiera's death was deemed a random act of violence. Now, Sarah lay in the ICU, in critical condition, unconscious and hooked to several monitoring devices due to another random act of violence.

"This don't make no goddamn sense," Eli mumbled angrily as he looked down at his mother's battered body.

Abe turned to face his brother. "It doesn't. What did Esau say?"

"Esau said he had no idea where Mama went."

"But why would Mama be in the JC Napier area? She hates that part of Nashville. It gives her hives just thinking about the projects," Abe stated.

"I know. Hell, it gives me the hives too," Eli turned up his nose in disgust. "Did you call Ike to tell him what's going on?"

Abe knew they would need to tell Ike sooner or later, but he didn't really want to disturb Ike on his much-needed vacation. Of course, when Ike found out, he would be upset with both Abe and Eli, but Abe was sure he'd get over it.

Abe said, "Naw, I'm not going to bother him just yet."

Esau walked into the room. He exchanged glances with both Abe and Eli. It was something about the way his eyes darted back and forth that didn't sit well with Abe.

"What took you so long getting here?" Abe wanted to know.

Esau shot Abe an angered look. "You don't question me."

"They called you two hours ago!" Abe's voice grew loud.

Eli gestured to Abe. "Be quiet. This is a hospital. You gon' get your ass put out."

Ignoring Eli, Abe walked upon Esau. "Why the fuck didn't you call me and Eli when they first called you?"

"I assumed you were called too," Esau answered casually.

A nurse walked into the room looking between the two men. She cleared her throat, "Only two at a time."

"I'm leaving," Abe said. He cut his eyes at Esau, "I can't be in the same room with this mothafucka anyway."

Eli looked at the nurse who seemed to be a little shocked. "Never mind him. He's a fool."

Before Abe walked away, he looked at Esau with eyes like ice. "Let me find out you got something to do with this. I'll personally beat the life out of you myself."

The nurse's eyes bulged out with alarm.

Eli offered the nurse a comforting smile. "He's just playing."

Lovely wasn't sure of which she should be more concerned about: the news Abe was keeping from her or the awkward silent treatment he was giving her. The latter seemed to concern her the most. She felt so stupid for entertaining Cesar's foolish talk. If she'd put a final end to the conversation, Abe would not have caught them talking. And talking wasn't the issue. It was the whispers and how Cesar had been in her personal space. Lovely couldn't make out Abe's facial expression, but she heard the skepticism in his voice when he asked what was going on. Even after Cesar tried to assure Abe it was nothing, Lovely could sense Abe wasn't buying it.

"Are you going to tell me what's bothering you?" Lovely asked. They had been home for a while now, and he had yet to say anything to her. She followed him to the study and stood over him as he sat at the desk.

Abe looked at Lovely trying to figure out exactly what it was he saw earlier between her and Cesar. He always knew their relationship to be that of a big brother/little sister. Never, in over a year's time had Abe ever suspected any romantic ties between them. But what he walked in on earlier didn't seem innocent. Then Cesar had the nerve to smirk. *What was that about?* Abe didn't like that at all.

"What were you and Cesar talking about?" He asked.

Lovely shrugged, "Nothing really."

"He was awfully close to you. Are you sure it was nothing?"

"I'm sure," she offered him a small smile. "Look, you ain't never been jealous; don't start acting like it now."

"It's not jealousy. It's just I need for him to know that he needs to respect the fact that you're my wife now. Being that close to you ain't necessary."

"It won't happen again. I'll be more mindful of it myself. Okay?" Lovely replied in a soft, soothing tone hoping to control the issue before it grew out of hand. "So, will you tell me what's bothering you about your mother?"

Abe was hesitant about telling Lovely anything. He didn't want her worrying. She was with child again; she didn't need the stress.

"Abe, tell me."

He exhaled heavily. "Promise me you won't get all frantic and shit."

"I won't."

"My mama is in the ICU at Vanderbilt."

Lovely gasped. "What? What happened?"

"See! You're already getting worked up."

"C'mon Abe, what's wrong with her? I have a right to know. She's my mother-in-law and AJ's grandmother."

"Right now she's in a coma. She was found in a bad part of the city; which is mind-boggling. I don't get it. They said she was attacked and no one saw anything. She was beaten badly and shot in the back," his voice lowered to a mumble when he added, "There was some brain hemorrhaging. She could die."

"Oh my God!" Lovely covered her mouth in shock. "Why didn't you tell me this sooner? Were you at the hospital earlier? I should've been up there with you. What's going to happen?"

Abe pulled Lovely down to his lap. "Baby, don't worry about any of that for now. Right now, I just want to make sure you and my kids are safe. These so-called random acts of violence have hit home twice in two weeks. I don't like it."

"I don't like it either," she jumped up from his lap. "We gotta make sure everyone is safe."

Abe pulled her back down and wrapped his arms around her waist to hold her down. "Everyone will be. And like I said, I don't want you getting all worked up about it."

"But baby—"

"No Lovely. Let me do all the worrying. You just stay put for a few days. I don't want you, the kids, Aunt Livy, Lulu or Robin leaving out of this house."

"Grace gotta go to school, Abe!"

"I'll take her, and I'll pick her up. If I gotta sit outside the school the entire time she's there, I'll do that too."

"Don't be silly," she caressed the side of his face. "Baby, are you okay?"

"I'm fine Love," he told her.

Lovely leaned over and kissed his forehead. "Don't worry. Everything will be fine. Sarah will wake up soon."

"I really hope so. I know I've been giving her the cold shoulder lately, but I'd hate for something to happen to her before we could mend our relationship," Abe said. He was glad Lovely couldn't see the water building in his eyes. The truth was, Abe was a mess on the inside. He had no idea what was going on. Everybody knew his damn secret, his half-brother was dirty and now possibly after his wife, and his mother was fighting for her life. *What more could go wrong?*

Chapter 4

Robin stirred from her sleep and took in her surroundings. There was a modest size flat screen television mounted on the wall that was tuned in to *Judge Mathis*. The volume was set low, and she could barely make out what the people in court were saying. If Judge Mathis was on, that meant it was past noon. *How long had she slept?*

Wincing from the brightness of the sun rays beaming in from the window's blinds; Robin sat up and realized where she was. She looked over to Eli who had become a permanent fixture at his mother's bedside. His soft brown eyes connected with hers.

She asked. "Have you slept at all?"

Eli shook his head. Robin could see he was tired, but he refused to leave Sarah's side, or get any sleep for that matter.

"Don't you wanna go home and get in your own bed? What about Bria and Bryce?" Robin asked.

"I'll be fine. The twins are in good hands with Lovely and Aunt Livy," Eli replied. His eyes went back to the television in the room.

"I'm here Eli. I can sit with your mother while you get some rest," Robin said.

"I'm fine," Eli assured her.

Robin got up from the reclining chair and walked to Eli. "You look so tired. I really wish you would leave with me and let me take care of you."

"Take care of me?" Eli asked. A devilish smile formed on his lips.

Robin smiled playfully, "Oh no. Don't get any ideas."

Eli looked Robin over with lustful eyes. His eyes lingered on the junction between her legs. "You know, it's been a minute since you let me hit that."

"That's because you were fucking Kiera. Don't try to get some now that she's gone," Robin told him.

"The two of us not fucking had nothing to do with Kiera," Eli replied.

Robin gave him a doubtful look. "Sure it wasn't."

Eli hooked his finger on the belt loop of Robin's jeans and pulled her to him. Grabbing a handful of her ass, he said, "I'll leave with you right now if you let me get some of this."

Robin shook her head, "You're a mess. You know that."

"I'm so serious."

Robin looked down at Eli with thought. Too bad she was loyal to Esau. She wouldn't mind making things work with Eli, but she was looking forward to the fabulous life Esau promised her. Besides, if it came down to it, Eli would have to be eliminated if he got in the way of their plans.

The sound of the door being pushed open caught their attention. Robin almost jumped out of her skin when she saw Esau enter the room. She moved away from Eli.

Esau looked from Robin to Eli. "What's going on in here?"

Eli's brow furrowed in aggravation. "What are you talking about?"

"I mean it looks like you were being inappropriate in your mother's hospital room," Esau said moving in closer. He shot Robin a look.

Eli looked at Esau like he was crazy. "We weren't doing anything except talking."

Esau looked at Sarah as the machines worked in a harmonious rhythm to maintain her life. She didn't even look like the same pretentious, pompous wife he knew. The endotracheal tube taped securely in her mouth took the focus away from her badly bruised and swollen face.

If only she hadn't been so determined to confront Esau with Robin; perhaps she would have lived a week longer. Even now with the possibility that Sarah could awaken and rat them all out was too risky. Sarah had to die. She was supposed to die. Esau was going to see to it that she died before she had the opportunity to open her eyes. The only issue standing in the way was being able to be in the room alone with her. Robin's job was to get Eli to leave. It looked to Esau as if she was trying to fuck him right in the hospital room.

Robin cleared her throat with uneasiness. "Uhm, Eli, I'll be back. I'm going down to the cafeteria for a minute."

As Robin was heading out, Mary, Sarah's sister, was heading in.

"Excuse me, baby. I didn't see you."

Robin brushed past her and exited the room. Eli made a mental note to understand why Robin always acted so frantic whenever Esau came around. It was weird.

Mary ignored Esau's presence and went straight to Eli. She hugged and kissed him. "I'm here sugar. You can go home now. I know them babies is missing their daddy."

"Are you sure?" Eli asked.

Mary nodded, immediately tending to her sister. "I wish she would wake up and tell us who did this to her."

"It's probably just some random thug," Esau said.

Mary cut her eyes towards him. "Who asked you anything? For all we know, your ass could have done this."

"Aunt Mary," Eli called out to calm her down.

"I'm with Abe on this," Mary said to Eli. "I don't trust that bastard."

Esau threw his hands in the air as if to surrender. "You know what? I'm not going to stand here and take your sick accusations."

Eli and Mary both watched as Esau stormed out of the room.

"Fuck his ass..." Mary hissed.

Esau looked around the hospital's cafeteria, making sure no one was around that he recognized before approaching Robin.

"What the fuck was that?"

"What was what?" Robin asked innocently.

Esau pulled her aside for more privacy as other people around them went about their business. “It looked like you were being a little too friendly.”

“I’m just playing the role, Esau,” Robin said.

Esau eyed her with suspicion. “Are you still fucking him?”

“No!” Robin exclaimed.

“He was rubbing all on your ass, Robin.”

“Again Esau, it’s the role. I still gotta show interest in him. It makes me look innocent in all of this.”

“Sure. Whatever,” he said sarcastically.

“So, you know Abe is tripping and tightening the security around the house. He’s paranoid.”

“What’s he saying?”

“Well, this is what Lovely has been telling me. He doesn’t want her or anybody else going anywhere. And it’s his idea to have someone that he trusts with Sarah around the clock.”

“So he doesn’t trust you to be alone with her?”

“Apparently not...”

Esau gave it some thought. “I wonder why. Have you ever done anything to show you weren’t trustworthy?”

Robin thought about the glares Abe would shoot her way whenever he caught her looking at him a little too long. “Nope. I guess he’s just really serious about all of this.”

“I gotta make sure Sarah doesn’t wake up,” Esau said.

“I’ll figure out something. But until then, we gotta play this cool.”

"Play it cool, huh? That means you gotta let my son play all in your ass?"

Robin didn't like the seriousness of the tone of his voice. "It's not like that Esau. I have no intentions of sleeping with Eli."

"If I find out you are, like I've said before, I will kick your ass."

Robin rolled her eyes at his statement, "Whatever Esau."

Esau sighed and looked around at the other patrons in the cafeteria. "We gotta get to Lovely. With Abe being so paranoid he's probably around more. Think of a plan to get her away from him, Robin."

The perfect idea instantly came to Robin. She smiled victoriously, "I know what'll definitely get Lovely away from Abe. She'll be left wide open."

An hour later, Eli was stopping by Abe's and Lovely's to get the twins before heading home. He was definitely tired, but it seemed as though he got a second burst of energy when he was surrounded by the kids.

"You know they're okay staying over here," Aunt Livy moved about in the kitchen cleaning up behind everyone.

"I know, but I've gotten used to them being in the house now," Eli said.

"But you need some rest," Lovely said from the breakfast nook. AJ thought Lovely speaking was the funniest thing. Lovely looked toward the bouncer that was propped on the table in front of her. “Why do you think everything I say is funny?”

A smile came to Eli’s face as he watched his three-month-old nephew laugh at his mother’s voice.

“Is he actually laughing?”

“He’s silly like his uncle,” Aunt Livy joked.

“He’s been laughing at me all day,” Lovely said. “I’m not thinking about AJ.”

Eli went to the table to observe AJ’s reaction to Lovely’s voice. It made him laugh. “He is really tickled.”

“I have a feeling he’s going to be just like you, mixed with a little Grace,” Lovely said. She started talking baby gibberish to AJ, getting him going even more.

Eli took a seat at the table with Lovely. “I want a little baby, but only if it’s like AJ. He’s a good baby.”

“Well, you and Robin need to stop playing around,” Aunt Livy said.

Lulu turned around from the task she was tending to at the other end of the kitchen and narrowed her eyes at Aunt Livy. “He no be with Robin, she not good.”

Eli was taken aback by Lulu’s bluntness. He chuckled, “Why you say that, Lulu?”

“She bad girl, I see it,” Lulu said.

Aunt Livy rolled her eyes and blew air in annoyance. “That China-woman don’t be talking with no sense.”

“I hear that,” Lulu sang out waving a finger at Aunt Livy.

“I wanted you to,” Aunt Livy retorted in a playful manner.

"You really want a baby Eli?" Lovely questioned.

He nodded, "Yeah, one day."

"What about marriage; are you ready to settle down?" she asked.

"I don't know. I guess with the right woman."

"And Robin isn't it, huh?" Lovely asked with a teasing grin.

"No, she isn't. I mean, she all right to kick it with. But it's something about her I don't quite connect with," he said.

"Yeah, that chemistry is important," Lovely said.

"You and my brother got good chemistry. That's what I want, y'all are just too damn perfect."

"I hate when people say that because we're not."

"Well, to us, y'all are. Y'all have perfect arguments and little fights and everything. But I'm so happy Abe found someone like you. You were made for him."

Lovely blushed at the compliment, "Ah Eli. You're so sweet when you wanna be."

"When I wanna be? I am sweet. Ask Robin," he joked.

Lovely slapped him playfully on the arm, "Ew... you're so nasty."

Eli looked at AJ staring back at him with curious, bright blue eyes. It was nice having the twins and becoming an instant father, but Eli did fantasize about experiencing fatherhood in the way his brother was able to. When thinking of a complete family, only one face popped into his head; Kris.

Eli lowered his voice and whispered to Lovely. "Is there something wrong with me if I find myself strongly attracted to this very not so girly girl?"

Lovely thought the question was silly. She tried not to laugh. "I wouldn't think so. What do you mean by not so girly girl?"

"Well, she don't look like you or Robin."

"So, what makes her not girly then; there's a lot of women that don't look like Robin or me."

"Yeah, but she looks like a little..." he let his voice trail off to come up with the right description, "...boy."

Lovely grunted a laugh causing AJ to start his own little giggling fit, "A boy?"

"Yeah, well, she's thin but muscular, like she works out. She used to wear her hair like really short, like a boy, but now she's growing it out in dreads. She don't wear girly clothes. It's always something baggy."

"Who is this person?"

"You haven't met her."

"Will I ever? Do Abe know her?"

Eli answered carefully, "I don't know, and yes, Abe knows her."

"Does Abe know you're attracted to her?"

"No. The thing is; she used to work for Abe, and everybody thought she was a lesbian."

"And she isn't? How do you know she's not?"

Eli cleared his throat, "Because."

Lovely waited for him to finish his explanation. "Because what?"

"Lovely," Eli said sternly. He repeated, "Because."

Then it donned on Lovely what Eli was trying to tell her. “Oh!”

“Yeah,” Eli laughed.

“Oh,” Lovely said with more thought. “So, you’re feeling this girl huh?”

“Kinda.”

“No wonder you ain’t into Robin like that,” Lovely teased.

“Can I show you a picture of her?”

Lovely’s smile faded, and she looked towards Eli like he had lost his mind. Eli burst into laughter. “I love it when you do that!”

“Fuck you, Eli!” Lovely exclaimed. AJ started laughing again. Lovely’s smile returned. “See, he’s going to be just like you. He thinks that shit is funny too.”

Chapter 5

Robin knew exactly what needed to happen to get Abe away from Lovely. With him away, it would easier for them to pull off the kidnapping. All she had to do was get Lovely angry at Abe.

Robin made her way to Abe's study. It was where Aunt Livy said she could find Lovely. She wanted to execute the plan as soon as possible. When she got to the study, she found the door was slightly ajar. She was about to barge right in, but a muffled sound stopped her. Robin peeked in and had a wonderful view of the study's sitting area. With that, she also had a great view of Lovely being ate the fuck out from behind, by Abe.

Shit, Robin thought. The way Lovely's mouth was slightly gaped open, Robin could tell she was in pure bliss. Robin watched as Abe came up and planted kisses on Lovely's neck and whispered something in her ear. As he was doing this, he started undoing his jeans. Leaving Lovely bent over the back of the sofa, Abe positioned her perfectly for his entrance. Robin wanted to see his dick, but his hand was in the way as he guided himself inside of Lovely. She cried out louder than what she should have. Abe began to shush her as he started stroking her at an even pace. Lovely wasn't thinking about Abe and his insistence on her being quiet. The sound of Lovely's moans, along with the rhythmic slap of their thighs meeting was enough to excite Robin.

Robin found her pussy aching badly when Abe started aggressively pounding Lovely's pussy. Robin admired every maneuver of Abe's. He delivered a combination of dick strokes that were so intense, Robin could literally feel it in her pussy. He had Lovely trembling and twitching. *Damn,* Robin wished it was her instead of Lovely receiving all that dick; and then to watch the muscles in his ass flex. *Damn, damn, damn*!

The sound of someone clearing their throat startled Robin. She jerked her head in the direction of the sound. Lulu stared back at her with a chastising expression. Robin decided not to say anything. She simply walked away and headed to her bedroom.

Robin was turned on and needed the satisfaction of some good dick. Esau was available of course, but he wasn't going to do. She needed someone that would get nasty with it and be relentless. She called Eli.

"Hello," Eli answered groggily.

"Eli, what are you doing?" Robin asked eagerly.

"Trying to sleep, who is this?"

"It's Robin. Wake up. I need a favor."

"I'm out of favors for today. Call me back tomorrow," he hung up.

Robin looked at her phone as the screen flashed, indicating the call had ended, "Bastard!" She dialed him again.

"What!" He answered.

"Stop being an ass. I need some dick."

There was silence.

"Eli?"

"What did you say?" He asked.

"I said I need some dick. Can I come over there?"

There was hesitation as if he was giving it some thought.

Robin asked, "Oh, so you don't want no pussy now? What was that shit you were talking earlier?"

"Who said I don't want any?"

Robin smirked, "So, you're awake now?"

"Not really," he groaned. "Robin, I think I'm gonna have to pass."

"Why?" She asked in disbelief.

"Damn. Is it that serious?"

Images of Abe swarmed in her head. Eli was the next best thing. "Yes!"

"Okay. Let me tell you what you need to do. Go down there to Hustler's on Church Street and buy you one of them big, black, lifelike dicks with some vibrating action—"

"Eli!" Robin yelled impatiently. "Stop playing."

Eli chuckled. "I'm so serious. I can't help you tonight."

"You got somebody over there?"

"If I did, would I be talking to you about buying dicks at the sex store?"

"I hate you."

"Well, okay. Is that all?"

"Fuck you!" Robin said angrily before ending the call.

Grace couldn't understand for the life of her why her mother wouldn't let her have a phone. Everyone else in the seventh grade had one. She was the only one walking around phoneless. But she loved her I-pod. She used it to block out the world around her and to get lost in her own. Like now; she was blocking Robin out as she gazed out of the passenger side window. The scenery and traffic were more interesting than engaging in a conversation with her.

Grace felt her earbud being tugged out of her left ear.

"Do you hear me Grace?"

"Nope," Grace answered quickly returning the earbud to her ear.

Robin pulled it out again. "Perhaps if you left these out you could hear somebody. Now, I was asking if you wanted me to stop and get you something to eat. I'm in the mood for *Koi*. What about you?"

Grace made an unsure face. "I'm not really hungry."

"Okay. I thought I'd ask," Robin mumbled.

"Where's Abe?" Grace asked. "How come he didn't come and get me?"

"He was, but he had something to take care of at the last minute."

"Oh," Grace put the earbuds back in her ears. Her mind wandered. Her friend Ashli asked if she could come over for the weekend to her birthday party and sleepover. Something was up with the grown-ups in Grace's house, and Abe was being really weird. He didn't want any of them away from the house for too long. Grace wondered if he would give her a pass to attend Ashli's party.

Grace turned to Robin to ask her a question but noticed Robin had suddenly become engrossed in what was going on in the rearview mirror. Robin went for her phone which caused Grace to remove her earbuds entirely.

"What do you want?" Robin asked in a hushed tone into the phone. Her eyes darted back and forth from the road ahead to the rearview mirror.

"I'm not pulling over... Because... I'm not alone!"

Grace leaned over to get a look in the side-view mirror but couldn't see clearly. She would need to roll her window down.

"Fine, I'll pull over at the Taco Bell coming up... And stay in the car. I'll come to you."

Grace looked at Robin wondering what was going on. Robin glanced at Grace shocked to see that she had been listening to her.

"I thought you had your earbuds in."

Grace ignored her statement. "Uhm, I thought you said you wanted Koi, not Taco Bell."

"I'm just—mind your business, Grace. Okay?"

Grace mocked Robin and rolled her eyes. She remained quiet as Robin parked and got out. She went straight to the black on black Charger that pulled in behind them. Grace rolled the window down and looked into the side-view mirror. *Why was Robin acting so secretive?*

Robin was talking to the person on the driver's side, but Grace couldn't make out who it was. A few seconds passed by and the passenger side door opened. Grace could see Robin getting riled up about something. She could hear Robin telling the person to stay in the car. The person ignored Robin as they stepped out of the car fully.

Grace watched through the side mirror as the tall man sauntered his way towards Robin. He reminded Grace of a thug turned rap artist. He was wearing more jewelry than necessary. She could tell that even his mouth was blinged out. There was something familiar about him though. His tanned complexion, soft curly hair; his build—Grace couldn't exactly pinpoint it.

"Wassup, Babygirl," he said once he made it to her window.

Grace just stared at him. The teardrop tattoos on his face caught her attention. He was someone her mother would want her to steer clear of. Grace asked calmly, "Do I know you?"

He knelt beside the door so he could be more leveled with her. "You should."

Robin yelled, "Lo, this isn't the time or the place! Let me get her home."

Lorenzo shot Robin a dismissive look. He returned his gaze back to Grace. He was looking at his daughter for the first time up close and personal. He definitely could see some of his features, but she resembled Lovely more. And just like her mother, she was beautiful. Her soft brown eyes stared back at him, blankly.

"Why should I know you?" Grace asked.

"My blood runs through your veins. Your mama haven't told you; I'm your daddy."

Grace looked confused, "My daddy? Like, my real daddy?"

Lorenzo smiled, “Yeah Babygirl. I’ve been waiting to meet you.”

Grace just stared at him. No way was this dude was her daddy. No way. “No thank you, I already have a daddy.”

Looking as if he was insulted, Lorenzo asked, “Who? I know you ain’t talking about that bitch Abe. That mothafucka ain’t your daddy. I am!”

Grace smiled wryly, “Yeah. Whatever.”

Lorenzo scoffed with amusement, “Yeah, you got a smart ass little mouth.”

Robin returned to the car. Before getting in on the driver’s side, she said, “Uhm, we gotta go so if you could please excuse us.”

Lorenzo stood to his full height and glared at Robin. “Hold up. You don’t run shit. I’m tryna have a father-daughter moment and yo’ ass ruining it.”

“Get away from the car,” Robin ordered angrily. Under her breath, she said, “Tacky mothafucka.”

“What did you say?” Lorenzo asked. He looked at the other car, “Hey Unc! Control your bitch ‘fore I smack her in the mouth.”

“I wish you would lay a hand on me!” Robin dared.

Lorenzo headed to the other side of the car. Robin quickly jumped in the car and locked all the doors. She gave Lorenzo the middle finger as she pulled off.

Robin looked at Grace who was wearing a befuddled expression, “You all right over there?”

“Who were those people?” Grace asked.

"Oh, that was one of Abe's cousins," Robin answered nonchalantly.

"Abe's cousin?" Grace was confused. "So why did he say he was my daddy?"

Robin looked shocked at first, and then she let out a nervous laugh, "Oh girl, never mind that nut. He's just messing around with you."

Grace didn't say anything. She sat back and placed her earbuds back in her ears. Now she wondered who Robin had been speaking to in the car. *And why did Robin know this guy so well?* Grace never met that guy before. All kinds of thoughts played in her head.

When they got to the house, before getting out, Robin said, "Please don't mention any of that to your mama and especially to Abe. They would freak out."

"Yeah, booty face," Grace joked as she got out of the car.

Robin smiled, "That's my girl."

Later that night, before retiring to bed, Grace made her way to the study where she found Abe at his desk. He looked exhausted as he stared blankly at nothing in particular. He hadn't even realized Grace had entered the room.

"You look like you need to go to bed," Grace joked as she took a seat on the other side of his desk.

Abe's eyes shifted to Grace's face. "What are you doing in here? Shouldn't you be in bed?"

"Please," Grace waved off dismissively. "I'm not seven. I'm twelve. I can handle late nights."

“Sure you can. That’s why you’re late getting to school every morning.”

“I get there late because of you. You drive like Aunt Livy!” She laughed.

“I do not!” Abe countered with a laugh.

“You really do, but that’s neither here nor there,” Grace mumbled matter of factly. She straightened up and put her serious face on. “But listen, I came to talk to you about something.”

“What’s up?” He asked as he sat back in his chair.

Grace leaned forward. “Do you know anything about my real father? I mean, I’m sure you and Mama talked about it. She doesn’t tell me much about who he is.”

“I probably know as much as you,” Abe answered. “She said he was just some boy she met and never kept in contact with.”

“I wonder if he still lives here...” Grace said in thought.

Abe was confused. “Where is this coming from?”

“Well, this guy... He came up to me and said I was his daughter. Why would he say that?”

Completely taken aback, Abe leaned forward. “Say what now? What guy?”

“Robin called him Lo or something. He had a lot of tattoos. He cursed at Robin and threatened to hit her.”

Abe couldn’t believe what he was hearing. Words couldn’t describe how mad he was. “When was this?”

“Today, she told me not to tell you because you and Mama would freak out. Are you freaking out? I can kinda see it—”

Abe cut Grace off. "Don't say anymore 'cause I swear—I'm beating this nigga's ass!"

Grace was somewhat startled by Abe's anger being that she never ever saw him in such a state. She knew Abe could set it off from overhearing the grownups discussing what went down at the Labor Day party. Grace figured his muscles weren't just for looks. He had to put them to use every now and then.

Abe was thrown by what he had just heard. Lorenzo actually went there and told Grace that shit. Abe didn't even know how to answer her. "I'm not sure why he would say something like that, but clearly he's crazy. And as far as I'm concerned, you're my daughter."

"That's another thing. He said that you weren't. He called you a bitch too."

"This Lo person is my cousin, Lorenzo. Right now, he's not someone I want around you, AJ, or your mama. What else did he say?"

"Nothing, but Robin said he was just messing with me and not to pay him any attention."

Abe blew air in frustration. "Okay, tell me exactly what happened today, don't leave nothing out, every single detail."

Grace started from the time Robin picked her up from school all the way to the very moment of her coming to find him to tell him everything.

Abe pondered on what Grace was telling him. He added the details up; however, it didn't make much sense to him. At first, Abe thought Lorenzo had stalked Grace and Robin before approaching them. From what Grace was saying, Abe was seeing a totally different picture.

"Grace, don't mention any of this to your mother," Abe said, "None of it."

"I won't."

Chapter 6

It was after the annual fundraiser at the community center, Takes A Village. David's restaurant Batey's Kuntry Kitchen was full with the attendees of the fundraiser. Their appetites were in demand for some of his good southern entrees. The place was filled with roaring chatter as people found seats, mingled, and purposely displayed themselves for show. There was a pleasant family like tone in the atmosphere. It was like that always, and it was one of the reasons Lovely enjoyed dining there.

Lovely hadn't ever heard Abe laughing and enjoying himself so much before. Hearing his laughter left her with such a warm feeling. It assured her he was happy. Dealing with his emotional struggles all his life, she was elated that he was in a better place with himself.

"You two are terrible," Luciano stated shaking his head.

"Yes, they are," Lovely said. She took a bite of what was supposed to be her salad with ranch dressing. She found out quickly it wasn't what she asked for. She spat it out, "Gross!"

Eli burst into laughter all over again. That was a tell-tale sign of his guilt.

Lovely asked, "Eli did you do this?"

"No, Abe did that shit this time," Eli snickered.

"Baby, don't listen to him. I swear I didn't do that. I wouldn't dare do you like that," Abe said desperately.

Not convinced by his playful pleas, Lovely asked, "Abe, why would you put bleu cheese on my salad?"

"That wasn't me," Abe denied. He shot Eli a sneaky grin.

"Uh huh," Lovely murmured, "How about you go get me another one... with ranch dressing."

"Yes dear," Abe said playfully. He kissed her on the cheek before getting up.

Eli watched his brother take joy in waiting on Lovely. He wondered if he would have that same spirited attitude towards the woman he decided to settle down with. Eli asked, "Lovely, what do you do to keep my brother so wrapped around your finger?"

"He's definitely wrapped," Luciano teased.

"Ain't nothing wrong with that," Cece added. "Is there, Lu?"

Luciano chuckled, "I guess there isn't."

Lovely smiled. "You think I got your brother wrapped around my finger, Eli?"

"Uhm... yeah," Eli answered.

"Well, Ike will be next because I'm pretty sure Jackie is working her magic on him as we speak," Luciano joked.

"I need to call them and see how they're doing," Lovely said.

Cece sighed dreamingly, "I'm sure they're having a great time in Aruba."

"They're not in Aruba anymore," Eli said. "They're in Paris now. They'll be there a week and then move on to Milan I think."

"They're gonna love Milan!" Cece said excitedly.

Eli looked in the direction Abe had gone. He was now talking to Robin at the salad bar. Eli hadn't realized she was present. His thoughts didn't rest on Robin long because an unlikely trio of patrons entered the restaurant. "What the hell?"

"What is it?" Lovely asked.

The others at their table glanced in the direction Eli was looking.

"These assholes," Luciano mumbled with a roll of his eyes. "Can we ever catch a break from them?"

Eli eyed Lorenzo, Esau, and Aisha. It was very shocking to see her with the uncle and nephew pair. Eli looked over at Abe to see if he noticed them. As the waitress seated them, Lorenzo wore a smirk and looked their way.

"I hope they're not here to start trouble," Cece said.

"Who is it?" Lovely asked.

"It's my poor excuse for a father and my illiterate cousin," Eli spoke.

"Just don't bother them and hopefully they won't bother us," Lovely said calmly. Then she realized Abe wasn't at the table. "Where's Abe?"

"He hadn't noticed them yet," Eli said. Watching Abe and Robin, Eli felt there was a weird exchange going on between them. Their body language said it all. First Robin looked like she was angry at what Abe said, but now it was reversed. Robin even walked away with a victorious smile on her face.

"Aw hell," Eli whispered under his breath. He shook his head as Abe's gaze landed on Esau and Lorenzo. Eli shot up from his seat with Luciano following suit. Eli searched the place for David's assistance. David was already on it.

"Hey, hey," David spoke sternly but in a soothing tone. He grabbed Abe by the arm before Abe could even charge in their direction. "Not here. Let them be."

"Of all mothafuckin places to be, they wanna show up here," Abe said angrily as he allowed David to pull him further away.

"I know, but there are too many people here that would be horrified by your behavior if things jumped off," David argued. By this time, Eli and Luciano had joined the two men.

"Yeah, Abe," Luciano said. "Just let them be... this time."

Eli turned his lip up in disgust at Aisha who was smiling a little too big for him, "What the fuck you doing over there with them?"

"Don't talk to me," Aisha said loudly while still wearing her arrogant grin.

"Are you fucking Lorenzo or Esau?" Eli asked. This caused other patrons to turn their attention to them. Some even snickered at Eli's inquiry.

"Eli!" David exclaimed.

Ignoring David, Eli was baffled and asked, "What the fuck she doing over there with them?"

To Abe, it all made sense at that moment. Aisha had come to his office on behalf of Lorenzo or Esau.

"Abe, you see that shit?" Eli asked.

"Yeah, I see it," Abe mumbled. He turned away and headed back to Lovely.

"Are you okay?" Lovely asked with great concern as she felt Abe taking his seat next to her.

"Yeah," he said.

She could hear he was disturbed in his tone. "Just don't worry about them. Pretend as if they're not here."

"Yeah." Was all he said. Grace's laughter from two tables caught his attention. *Shit*, he thought. He looked back at Lorenzo, who happened to be eyeing Grace. "I think we need to go."

"Why? They're not bothering us," Lovely said.

"But we all just got here, Abe," Cece added.

Abe didn't say anything. He continued to look from Grace to Lorenzo. If Lorenzo so much as smiled at Grace to make her uncomfortable, Abe knew he wasn't going to be able to contain his anger.

Luciano returned to their table and took his seat beside Cece. "Abe, you okay?"

Abe nodded. Luciano could see the unhinged look in Abe's eyes. His son had a very intense hatred for Esau and Lorenzo. Luciano was beginning to think there was more to the story behind all of this anger than Abe let him know. He made a mental note to get to the bottom of it.

Later that night, giving Eli and Mary a break, Lovely and Robin decided to check in on Sarah and sit with her for a while.

Robin let out a bored sigh. "Why is it necessary to sit with this woman every day again? Can you explain this to me?"

Annoyed with Robin's lack of compassion, Lovely said, "If you were in a coma, would you want people to care enough about you to check on you?"

"So, you care about this lady?" Robin asked flippantly.

"She's my mother in law. She's AJ's grandmother. Furthermore, she's my husband's mother; despite what kind of relationship they have had in the past. Robin, what's gotten into you? You used to be a little bit kinder than this. Like, when your own mother was going through her own illness."

Robin blew out a frustrated breath and took a seat in one of the chairs in the hospital room. "I don't know. I just got some things on my mind."

"Like what?" Lovely asked.

"Nothing you could help me out with," Robin mumbled.

"Is it man problems?"

"Of course not," Robin replied. "Fuck men."

Lovely rolled her eyes in exasperation. "Here we go."

"Oh shut up, Lovely. What would you know with your perfect little life?"

Lovely slightly. "What makes you think my life is so perfect, Robin? I mean, haven't you been around long enough to know that I've gone through some things?"

"But everything still ends up laughed perfect for you."

"And you don't think you'll have the same fate?"

Robin thought about her plans with Esau, and a wicked smile crept across her face. "Yeah, I think I will. It's just getting there."

"It'll come. But until then, let's work on your attitude, Miss."

Robin rolled her eyes upward and mocked Lovely. She looked at Sarah lying motionless in the hospital bed. *Why don't you die already*?

Lovely turned her attention back to Sarah and gently rubbed her hand. She spoke softly. "I know you don't know this lady, but your son is really messed up behind all of this. I would love nothing more for you to come out of this so that you and Abe can finally have the relationship you two deserve with each other. He really needs you. It would make him complete."

Hearing this was amusing to Robin. "Oh, so now Abe likes his mama?"

"Robin, really?" Lovely snapped her head in Robin's direction. "What's wrong with you?"

Robin shrugged, "Nothing. It's just that last week Abe couldn't stand Sarah. Now that she's half dead, he likes her; how convenient."

"Robin, keep your negative thoughts to yourself. Please," Lovely said with irritation.

"No. I'm tired of keeping my *negative* thoughts to myself. I know I've asked you this before, but as always you come up with some evasive response to shut me up. But how well do you know Abe?"

"What are you getting at, Robin?"

"I'm getting at the fact that Abe isn't as good as you think."

"Oh really?" Lovely turned to face Robin completely. "What is it that you think you know, Robin?"

"I know that he has eyes for other women. But of course, this is something you can't see for yourself," Robin said. She enjoyed the look of doubt flooding Lovely's face.

"He's a man. He should look at other women. It wouldn't be normal if he didn't," Lovely responded confidently.

"Yeah, that's true, I guess. But these looks are like little conversations. Conversations he can't have with you I might add."

Lovely was becoming a little agitated. "What conversations?"

"Like, *let's hook up* conversations," Robin said. She tried to hide her smile, but this was so much fun for her. "Look, Lovely, I wouldn't be a true friend if I didn't tell you the things I see and know for myself."

"What do you mean know for yourself?" Lovely asked.

"Well, he's been inappropriate with me a few times," Robin tried her best to sound hurt and disappointed in Abe's actions.

"Inappropriate, how?"

"Being flirty, brushing up against me and making little gestures... you know; stuff like that," Robin said.

Lovely could no longer pretend as if the things Robin was saying didn't affect her. They did, and she could feel herself getting hot from the rise in her temperature.

"How long has this been going on?"

"With me? Since the two of you started seeing each other." Robin lied.

"And you're just now saying something?" Lovely asked angrily.

Gotcha! Robin thought. "Well, you seemed so happy with him. I didn't wanna ruin that for you."

"But now you tell me! After I've married him and had a baby with him!"

"I know Lovely. I shoulda said something way sooner," Robin said apologetically.

"You think!" Lovely exclaimed. "So, what else do you know Robin?"

"Well," she tried to think of more lies. "I didn't want to say anything, but I caught him and Kiera in a compromising position before she died. And then Eli told me in so many words that Abe still gets down with his exes."

"What!" Lovely stood up and marched towards the door.

"Where are you going?" Robin called after her.

"Take me home!"

"But don't you have to..." Robin's voice trailed off as Lovely disappeared into the hallway. She snickered devilishly to herself as she got up to follow behind her.

The sun dipped below the horizon cascading a glow of orange rays across the sky. The view was peaceful, calm, and tranquil. Abe wished his life still mimicked nature's mural before him. He felt like he was losing control over his own life. If he could just get things back to the way they were. He was at peace before Lovely, but he was without love. Furthermore, he was without his son. So, no, he didn't want to go back that far, because he couldn't imagine his life without his family. But he needed control.

"Son," Luciano started. He placed his hand on Abe's shoulder as he held a glass of cognac in the other. "You seem pretty tense. Are those knuckleheads from earlier still bothering you?"

Abe continued to gaze out into Luciano's backyard as they, along with others, stood outside on the back terrace. "Yeah, something like that."

"You know I'm here for you. Just give me the word, and I can have them taken care of," Luciano said in a serious tone.

Abe looked at Luciano with a questioning look. His lips spread into a smile. "You would do that for me?"

"Of course. Besides, I've been wanting a reason to handle that Esau."

Abe gave it some thought. "I'm trying not to go there in my actions."

"Sometimes you have to do what you have to do," Luciano said as he raised one eyebrow.

Just then, Cesar walked over to join the two men, "Hey Papa. I think I'll be heading on out."

"Okay. As always, son, be safe." Luciano said as he turned his attention to Cesar.

Abe eyed Cesar suspiciously. Cesar's whole vibe didn't sit right with Abe anymore; especially since Ike told him he saw

Cesar speaking to Lorenzo at the Labor Day party. He still wanted to get to the bottom of why he had been so close to Lovely.

"See you brother," Cesar said to Abe.

"Yeah," Abe said in a careless manner.

Antino walked over to Abe and put his arm around his shoulder. "Let me have a word with you for a second."

Abe groaned. "I'm not trying to deal with no bullshit right now."

"I'm not bullshitting you, Abe," Antino chuckled. He put enough distance between them and the others, so no one could hear their conversation. "So, I see you're not feeling your brother much."

"Something's up with that mothafucka," Abe eyed Cesar laughing it up with Luciano's other guests. He looked back at Antino. "Why didn't you tell me he was the one that set up the shit against Lovely's father?"

"So he told you?" Antino wasn't shocked; more so amused.

"Yeah. From what he told me, Mano contacted him about the people that killed Lovely's parents. That's when he admitted to me that he was the one that went through you to hire us. Why?"

"He didn't tell you why?"

"No."

Antino scoffed as in deep thought.

"Why would he do that? Wasn't Lu and Lovely's daddy good friends? What about Ahkil and Mano?" Abe wanted to know.

"Mano has no idea about the goings on his brother was dealing in. And although Ahkil had problems with Dharmesh that stemmed from years ago when he decided to marry Lovely's mother, Naomi, he would never want his nephew, and his family harmed. Of course, their marriage went against their tradition. But Ahkil trusted Dharmesh with the family business. "

"Hold up, hold up," Abe interrupted. "What are you saying? What family business?"

Antino lowered his voice even more. "Dharmesh wasn't just into convenience stores. That was his front. He was the biggest money launderer there was. He moved millions. The money we stole that night wasn't even his. Guess whose it was?"

"Whose?"

Antino turned his gaze to Luciano.

"What?" Abe asked in disbelief. "I stole my daddy's money?"

Antino nodded.

"And you participated in robbing your brother?" Abe asked.

"I didn't know it was Lu's money until after."

"But you were willing to go along with killing your brother's best friend," Abe said as he shook his head in disgust. "I can't believe this shit, Ant."

"Dharmesh was getting beside himself. He was becoming too powerful and convinced Lu not to consider me in partnership with him. So yes, I was on some get back shit. So was Cesar. Besides, Dharmesh had been running his mouth to the feds."

"Dharmesh?"

Antino noticed Luciano coming their way. He said under his breath, "Remember, I said everybody isn't what they portray to be."

Chapter 7

The following day, Eli was excited to be in Kris' company again. He told himself that he would finally tell her how he felt. If he could, he was going to try to convince her to stay.

Kris showed up looking very different than she was the last time Eli laid eyes on her. The short dreads were styled into a nice pinned-up up-do that accentuated her femininity. She was also wearing a peach colored tank with a long, peach, tie-dyed maxi skirt with gold, thong gladiator sandals. Eli had to blink several times to make sure he was seeing her image correctly.

"Hey," Kris smiled brightly as she moved in closer for a hug.

"Hey," Eli wrapped his arms around her and held her tight. He released her, stepped back, and took in the sight of her. "You look different... again. Are you gonna make up your mind who you wanna be?"

"Well, I'm just exploring different looks as I explore different aspects of myself," Kris said. "I'm on a different journey in life now, Eli. All thanks to Yahweh."

"Girl, I don't wanna hear none of that Erykah Badu shit!" Eli blurted, "Getcho ass in this house and leave that Buddha shit out here."

Kris was tickled as she stepped across the threshold to Eli's home. She followed him upstairs to the main level of the house.

"Can I get you anything?" Eli turned to face her to catch her looking around as if she was expecting someone, "Who the hell you looking for?"

"Where are the kids?" Kris asked.

"I let them sit over my brother's house for a while," he said.

Kris nodded as she took a seat on his sofa in the den. "I guess I could use a drink."

"Like what?"

Kris shrugged, "Whatever you got."

Eli gave her a playful look, "Alright. I'll get you drunk in this bitch. Then I can do all kinds of things to you."

Kris shot him a devious smile, "I ain't gotta be drunk for that to happen."

"Well, how about we skip the drink for now and go ahead and get it poppin?"

"Boy, don't play," Kris laughed. "I didn't come over here for that."

Eli stood behind the sofa and looked down at her. "What did you come over here for then?"

"To see you and spend some time with you," Kris said.

Eli smiled down at her. "You miss me, Kris?"

"Of course I do," she said softly.

Eli walked around the sofa and reached out for her hand. Kris placed her hand in his and allowed him to pull her up. "Come with me," he told her.

Kris didn't say anything as she followed him into his bedroom. He made her sit down on his bed. Kris watched in surprise as Eli knelt to remove her sandals. That was something he had never done before. He even kissed her toes. A smile crept across her face. "Eli, what are you doing?"

"Don't say nothing... before I realize what I'm doing and stop," he planted kisses up her legs as he pushed her skirt up along the way.

Kris' heartbeat quickened. "Eli?"

"Shut up!" Eli commanded.

"Okay," Kris said. His hands found their way to her panties, and he began to tug at them. I *know he's not about to do what I think he's about to do*, Kris thought as she watched him lower his head in between her thighs. "Eli!"

Eli popped his head up and sighed with annoyance, "Dammit Kris! Do you want me to eat your pussy or not?"

"But you've never done that before," Kris said as she wore a silly grin.

"To you, I haven't. But I know how to eat pussy. I would like to show you if you shut the hell up!"

"But you've *never* done it," Kris reiterated.

Eli propped his arm up on his elbow and rested his face in the palm of his hand. He looked at Kris with very little patience. "You're killing my vibe right now. I'm in the mood for pussy eating, and you gotta keep reminding me that I've never tasted your twat."

"Okay. Go ahead," Kris said as she leaned back on her forearms and closed her eyes.

"I don't wanna do it now," Eli said and stood to his full height.

Kris' head jerked up. "Oh, stop that Eli. Come on."

"Nope, you've killed the damn mood," Eli pouted as he sat down beside her.

Kris traced her finger along his ear and whispered, "I'm sorry, baby. What do I need to do to get you back in the mood?"

Eli slapped her hand away, "Nothing."

Kris went back to tracing her finger along his face. "I missed you, Eli," she leaned over and nibbled at his earlobe. From there she caressed his neck with her lips and gently sucked. She whispered. "Do you miss me?"

"Actually, I do,"

Kris maneuvered her body in front of his as she kissed his lips softly. "You do?"

Eli nodded. He returned her kisses and pulled her onto his lap. "I wanna show you how much."

"Then show me," Kris challenged. Before she knew it, Eli had flipped her over on her back and had her skirt pushed up around her waist. With her legs resting on his shoulders, he dove in for dining.

Kris gasped and let out a soft moan. The sensation of Eli's tongue sensually exploring the folds of her pussy drove her quickly to the edge.

"Oh, Eli baby," she grabbed the comforter on his once neatly made bed. She tried to resist the urge to touch his head, but she rotated her hips in rhythm to his tune, "Just like that... oh God, Eli!"

Eli's phone started ringing in his pocket.

Don't answer that, Kris was thinking as she felt herself nearing orgasm. *Please don't answer that.*

Ignoring the violent ringing of his phone, Eli persisted in his quest to bring satisfaction to Kris. He wouldn't let up no matter how much his phone demanded his attention.

Kris' breathing deepened, and her hands cupped the back of Eli's head as she thrust against the stiffness of his tongue. She felt a need to make an announcement.

"I'm about to cum!"

The phone rang again just as Kris let out a long wail as she was pushed over the edge. Her body trembled and jerked in response to her explosive orgasm.

Eli answered his phone. "What?"

"For real, Eli!" Abe barked in the phone.

"What nigga? I answered the damn phone."

"I ain't talking about you answering the phone. I'm talking about this shit you done told Robin about me."

"What shit?"

"Bring your ass over here!" Abe demanded before hanging up the phone.

Eli looked at his phone with confusion. "What the fuck!"

With her breathing regulated, Kris asked. "What is it?"

"My brother tripping with his cockblocking ass," Eli said. He looked down at Kris and could see a glow on her face. He smiled at her. "He just gon' have to wait. I got my own business to tend to."

Kris smiled, "Oh yeah. And what's that?"

Instead of answering that, Eli asked. "Can I tell you something, Kris?"

"What Eli?" Kris prepared for something sarcastic to come out of his mouth.

"I love you."

That completely threw her off. "What?"

He kissed her softly and tenderly on the lips and repeated. "I love you."

Lovely sat on the edge of her bed with her arms folded. Her face was tight, and she was trying to get her breathing under control. She didn't think it would but throwing clothes out of the closet was tiring.

"You're doing all of this for nothing," Abe said.

"So Robin is lying on you and Eli?" Lovely asked angrily.

"Yes! The bitch is jealous of you Lovely. She wants what you got," Abe argued.

"Hold up. So, I'm a bitch now?" Robin asked as she leaned against the wall.

"You know what the fuck you are," Abe said to her. His earlier conversation with Robin replayed in his head. She was doing all of this because she was afraid Abe would go to Lovely with what he discovered about Robin. He gave Robin the chance to come clean about stealing money from Lovely, but instead, she threatened him with revealing his other secret. Abe was willing to play along with her, but he had no idea she was going to pull this shit.

Robin's smirk said it all. Right now, she had the upper hand. "Lovely, I wouldn't make any of this up."

"Lovely, listen to me. I would never do something like that to hurt you, baby," Abe pleaded.

"Oh, you wouldn't?" Robin questioned.

Abe really wanted to choke her to death at this point. He could just eliminate her ass, and that would be one last person to worry about.

"You need to shut the fuck up."

"That's the problem. I've been quiet for too long. I'm not gonna sit back and watch you disrespect Lovely behind her back, and sometimes in front of her," Robin said maintaining her act.

"Why are you still in here?" His patience for her was running very low.

"Because, I know how you men are," Robin sneered. "You'll be in here trying to convince Lovely that I'm lying, and sweet talk your way out of this."

"Well, let that be something Lovely decides," he stepped closer to Lovely, "Baby, can you—"

"Abe, just leave," Lovely said calmly. "Just leave and let me think about this."

"There's nothing to think about. I didn't do this shit she's talking about; if anything—"

Robin cleared her throat in an exaggerated manner to get Abe's attention. He looked at her with murderous eyes. Robin felt very proud of herself and was thinking of the praise she would get from Esau and the crew for pulling this off.

"You know what Lovely," Abe said as he began picking up his clothing. "I'll leave for the night. But when I come back tomorrow, I hope you've come to your senses."

Lovely ignored him. She looked away as he prepared to leave. As he made his way to the door, Robin suddenly started screaming which startled Lovely.

"Lovely!" Robin screamed out as Abe jerked her by her hair. He had her head pushed down as he spoke to her.

"Bitch, when I get back, you need to be gone!" He said through clenched teeth.

"Abe!" Lovely got up to go to Robin's aide.

Abe released Robin with a push. She stumbled back and looked at him in fear. "Are you serious?"

"I'm very serious. You better realize who the fuck you fucking with," Abe threatened.

"Abe, just go," Lovely insisted.

"You see how violent he is," Robin replied. "I'm surprised he doesn't go around killing people's parents and shit of that nature."

Abe reached for Robin's throat this time, but Lovely got in between them before he could grab her. Lovely cried, "Abe! Stop it. Just go. Leave!"

"You better be glad Lovely care enough about you. Can you say you care the same about her?" Abe asked Robin.

"Leave, Abe!" Lovely demanded.

Robin waited until Abe exited the room. "Do you believe me, Lovely?"

"I don't know," Lovely said in a low tone.

"You see his violent outbursts against women," Robin said. "You don't need that."

Lovely had to admit that was a side of Abe she hadn't witnessed before. She wouldn't have believed him to lay a finger on a woman. She realized he had a violent past, *but against women?*

There were several things that bothered Lovely about all of this. One being the comment Robin made about killing people's parents. It made Lovely think back to the odd way Kenya acted at Kiera's repast. Secondly, *did Lovely honestly believe Abe was cheating on her?* Although it was something that crossed her mind once before; as of late, Lovely had been very secure in her marriage with Abe. He had given her no reason to think otherwise.

"Robin, can you give me a minute?" Lovely needed space to gather her thoughts.

"Sure. Just call for me if you need me." Robin said. She walked out of the room wearing a wicked grin. That was so easy.

Kris was in heaven as she lay in Eli's arms. They had just made love and were relishing the moment. She smiled.

"So, where do you want to go from here?"

"I want you to come back here to live with me," Eli said.

"Are you sure?" Kris asked.

"Yeah,"

"Well, I need some time to make the move. I need to find another job here."

"Oh, don't worry about that. I got you covered. Shit, you don't have to work. You can keep Lovely company all day. That can be your job."

"Lovely wouldn't want me up under her all day."

"She wouldn't mind. She would enjoy your company."

"How do you know?"

"That's my sis in law. Lovely's cool."

There was silence. Kris needed to tell Eli what she had been holding in for all this time. She just didn't know how to say it without angering him. Carefully she said, "Eli, remember when I said I had something to tell you?"

"Yeah, I remember. What is it?"

"First, I wanna make sure you won't be mad at me."

"I won't, Kris. Just spit it out."

Kris opened her mouth to speak, but another voice boomed across the room.

"Eli! Didn't I tell your punk ass to come over to my house?" Abe shouted angrily.

Eli sat up and was shocked to see his brother standing in his bedroom doorway, "What the hell you doing here?"

"Who the fuck you got in here?" Abe walked further into the room.

"None of your business, get outta my room!" Eli ordered.

Kris stayed tucked securely under the covers as she meekly looked up into Abe's eyes.

"Kris?" Abe asked in disbelief.

Kris gave him a small wave. "Hey."

Abe looked at Eli flabbergasted, "You fucking Kris?"

"You fucking Lovely?" Eli retorted smartly.

Abe cut his eyes at Eli. He headed for the door and called over his shoulder, "You got thirty seconds to meet me out here in this hallway."

"What the fuck!" Eli groaned. "This better be for a good reason; marching in here like you own the damn place. Nigga, this my house! I don't be barging in on you and Lovely when y'all making babies and shit."

"Do you want me to come in there and snatch you out of that bed?" Abe asked.

Eli could hear his voice, but he couldn't see Abe. "You might get a bruise to your ego and be a little intimidated if you snatch me out of this bed. You'll see the biggest dick you've ever seen."

Kris giggled as Eli proceeded to throw his pants back on.

"I've seen your dick, Eli," Abe chuckled. "It's the same size it was when you were eight."

"Whatever," Eli said as he joined Abe in the hallway. He was greeted by a smack on his head.

With widened eyes, Eli looked at Abe like he was crazy, "Is you crazy?"

"Are you?" Abe responded. He slapped Eli again. "What the hell you been telling Robin?"

Recovering from the second slap, Eli said, "I ain't been telling her anything."

Abe slapped Eli with his other hand. "Why the fuck she telling Lovely you told her I'm still messing around with Aisha and Kenya?"

Eli prepared for another slap and guarded himself. "I ain't told Robin no shit like that!"

Abe went to hit him again, but Eli blocked it. "Look now! You ain't gonna keep on hitting me!"

Abe hit him anyway. Eli smacked Abe back which lead to them slapping each other like two little boys. Abe finally had enough and twisted Eli's arm and shoved him into the wall. Eli hollered out in pain.

"So, you didn't tell Robin anything like that?"

"No!"

"Why didn't you bring your ass over to my house like I told you to?"

"You see I've been fucking Abe, damn! Can you let me go?"

Abe sniffed, "Nigga, you been eating pussy?"

Eli chuckled, "Why you smelling me? Yeah, I've been eating pussy. Kris flavored pussy."

Abe released Eli but not before slapping him again.

"Mothafucka!" Eli growled before going after Abe.

Chapter 8

As much as Robin pretended she didn't like it at first, she was enjoying the way she was being dicked down. She hadn't gotten dick this good since Eli's wild ass.

She cried out with each forceful thrust. She held on tight to her lover as he pounded away in her pussy. She sat on the kitchen counter with her legs wrapped around his waist, receiving the punishment he delivered.

"You like this dick, bitch?" He asked.

"Yes!" She panted.

"I like this sweet pussy too," he said. "You acted like you didn't want to give me this—Bitch, gimme this pussy and tell me how much you like this dick!" He dug deeper until she was crying out in pain.

"This dick is so good," she whimpered.

"That's what the fuck I thought," he quickened the pace, pummeling her. Robin took it like a champ all the way until he gave three last hard pumps as he busted his seeds inside her.

"Goddamn that was good," she admitted with a smile.

"It sho in the fuck was," he smiled as he backed up from her.

Robin was about to say something until she noticed they weren't alone. Looking past Lorenzo made him turn around to look also.

"Really, Lo?" Aisha stood in the space that separated the entryway from the living room, which gave her a clear view of the kitchen.

"Really Lo my ass," Lorenzo said as he pulled up his jeans. "How 'bout the fuck you knock next time?"

"Why would I have to when you gave me a key," Aisha glared at Robin. "Really, bitch? I thought we were girls."

Robin hopped down from the counter and retrieved her panties and jeans. "We ain't never been girls."

"Oh yeah, so what would Esau think of this?" Aisha asked haughtily.

"Mind your fucking business," Lorenzo sneered.

"Y'all just a bunch of low life scum," Aisha shook her head in disgust.

"And what the fuck that make you?" Lorenzo retorted, "You hanging with us, hoping to get a piece of the pie."

"So why are you fucking Robin?" Aisha asked angrily.

"Why are you asking a fucking stupid ass question?" Lorenzo walked past her and made himself comfortable on the sofa.

Now that she was dressed, Robin headed for the bedrooms. "I'll be back here if y'all need me."

"Tramp," Aisha said loud enough for Robin to hear her.

Robin ignored her.

Aisha walked over to where Lorenzo sat. He casually channel-surfed on the big screen television before him. "So, it's like that Lo?"

"We ain't going together, Aisha. You ain't my woman, and I ain't your man."

"You could have fooled me," Aisha took a seat next to him.

"If your ass 'bout to yap at the fuckin mouth, you might as well go on and get away from me. I ain't tryna hear that shit right now."

"I'm not. This will be the last time you see me or hear from me. I quit this shit. I'm out," she said.

"Bitch!" Lorenzo backhanded Aisha in the mouth. "What the fuck you say?"

Aisha cried out in pain as she held her mouth. She looked at her hand and saw she was bleeding. "Lo! Why did you do that?"

"What makes you think I'm some nice mothafucka who wanna listen to this bullshit?" He spat. "You ain't quitting shit unless I say you can; you in this shit deep. You hear me?"

Aisha was still stunned by Lorenzo's smack to her face.

"Bitch, you hear me talking to you!" Lorenzo screamed at her.

For fear of being hit again, Aisha nodded as tears began to flow from her eyes.

"Shut the fuck up and fix me something to drink." He turned his attention back to the television.

Aisha got up and headed to the kitchen. She paused long enough to lock gazes with Robin who appeared back at the hallway's entrance. Robin wore a smug smirk as she turned away from her.

Aisha thought to herself, *I got a trick for their asses.*

Lovely awakened to the brightness of the sun painted against her face. It made her smile. Another day to live and enjoy what life had to offer.

Feeling him shift behind her as he normally did during his morning stretch put a smile on her face. He poked her in the ass with his morning stiffness. She wondered if he wanted her to ride it this morning or if he would just get it from the side.

She got her answer when she felt him forcing his way in from behind.

"I know you're awake," Abe said quietly. "So open up and let me in."

Lovely smiled as she helped to guide him to her love tunnel. She was wet and ready as if they hadn't made love all night.

He whispered in her ear, "*Te quiero tanto amor. Yo no quiero estar lejos de ti nunca más.*"

He said those words to her the night before when he returned home. He told her how much he loved her and how he didn't want to be away from her, ever. A part of Lovely was overjoyed inside when Abe came right back home. He wasn't going to just walk away for no reason. She appreciated that about him. It made her feel as though she was an important part of his life. He had shown up with Eli as they tried to convince her that Robin was lying on them. Lovely believed Abe and Eli. *But where did that leave her with Robin?*

Thirty minutes later, Abe put Lovely back to sleep. He lay there with his eyes closed as the thoughts flowed through his head. *How in the hell did Robin know about his past? And how long had she known? Could he trust Cesar? Was Antino telling the truth? Did Lovely know her father was a criminal? What did Luciano know? Who attacked his mother? What in the hell did Lorenzo have up his sleeve?*

"Ahem."

Abe opened his eyes to see Robin standing over him. He made sure he was covered properly. He looked over at a sleeping Lovely to make sure she wasn't disturbed. He looked back at Robin and whispered, "What the fuck you want?"

"I don't know what you did, but next time, it won't work."

"How about you get out of my goddamn room, you sneaky bitch…" Abe responded.

Robin gave him a wicked grin as she turned to walk out of the room.

This bitch got me fucked up, Abe thought as he jumped out of bed. It took him all of thirty minutes to shower and throw on some comfortable clothes. He went in search of Robin. He found her in her bedroom.

"What's up with you?" Abe asked.

Robin sat on her bed and smiled arrogantly, "Nothing."

"Why are you trying to cause trouble for me and Lovely? You're supposed to be one of her best friends. Why would you want to hurt her?"

"Hurt her? I see it as I'm doing her a favor."

"By stealing her money?"

"Like I told you at the restaurant, Lovely knew about my foundation," Robin replied.

"She did? So, what was the reason for you bringing up my past?"

"That's just something I believe she should know."

"So you make up lies instead. Something doesn't seem right about any of this, Robin. You got information on me that could guarantee Lovely would hate me forever, but instead, you choose to make up some stupid shit to tell her."

Robin didn't answer as she pretended to be enthralled by her phone's content.

"I tell you what, Robin," Abe said coolly. "Get out of my house, and I let you live."

Robin started laughing, "Really Abe? You really wanna threaten me right now?"

"I'm giving you until noon to be out of here."

"Or what? Lovely ain't gonna let you put me out."

"Well, wait until noon and let's see."

Robin made sure Abe was gone before dialing Esau.

"Hello?"

"So, this fucka wants to put me out!" She said angrily.

"Who?"

"Abe,"

"But I thought you took care of him last night?" Esau said.

"I did, but he came back. Now Lovely's probably thinking differently of me."

"Is Lovely putting you out?"

"She doesn't know."

"Well, talk to her about it. If she says it's okay for you to remain there, then that's just one more thing for them to argue about."

"I guess. When are we gonna make the move?" Robin asked impatiently. "It seems like y'all ain't serious."

"Robin, we just gotta make sure everything is perfectly aligned."

"What's to it? Just kidnap the bitch and hold her for ransom. We get our money, and we all bounce. What's so hard about that?"

"Let me make a phone call. You just work on Lovely," Esau ending the call.

Robin took in deep breaths as if she was about to hyperventilate. She forced tears to come to her eyes. She had to look the part. She had to be distraught about Abe attacking her and putting her out the house. Here goes nothing.

Aisha knew she was not welcomed, but she had to see Abe. Wearing dark Chanel sunglasses, she strolled inside Southern Wild nightclub. It was a weekday; therefore, it was hardly any clubbers in the building; however, the relaxed, sophisticated atmosphere was still present.

As she stood there, looking around, one of the barmaids came up to her.

"Can I help you?"

"I'm looking for Abe Masters."

The girl pointed up to the second floor. "He's up there. Just go to the left, and they're all sitting at the table. You can't miss them."

"Okay," Aisha headed in that direction. She didn't know why Abe wanted to meet her here. Hell, she was surprised he agreed to meet her at all after their last run in.

As the girl stated, Aisha found Abe sitting at a table amongst others, on the second floor of the club. Before she even made it to the table, Eli was already giving her the evil eye. She didn't have time for him tonight. She was there on some genuine shit.

"Hey Abe," Aisha said nervously. She ignored Eli's turned up nose.

"Have a seat," Abe directed.

"Could we possibly talk somewhere private?" Aisha asked.

Abe looked around the table at his crew, "Whatever you have to talk to me about you can say it in front of them. In fact, I rather have it this way. You know... to ensure your safety."

Aisha knew he was referring to the gun incident. She sighed and took a seat in the vacant chair next to him. She waved the smoke coming from their cigars and blunts away from her face.

"What's with the sunglasses?" Eli asked.

Aisha flipped her hair in his face as a reply. "Look, Abe, I think something is about to go down."

"I'm listening," he waved his hand that held the cigar for her to continue.

"It's Esau and Lorenzo. I don't know exactly, because they don't tell me everything. All I know is, I believe Lovely is in danger."

"What makes you say that?"

"Because they said it."

Eli studied her face, closely. "You've been getting Botox?"

Aisha shot Eli a look.

"I'm just saying. Your lips look swollen like you've been stung by bees. Did the bees sting you? Is you that sweet the bees mistook your lips for honey?" Eli taunted.

"Fuck you, Eli," Aisha said in annoyance.

"Eli, leave that girl alone," Eric laughed.

"Why are you here telling me all of this now?" Abe asked. "Just the other day you were sitting with Esau and Lorenzo like you were sitting amongst kings or something."

"I was just stupid, Abe," Aisha said sincerely.

"You fucked Lorenzo?" Abe asked.

"What does it matter?"

"Aisha, I never thought you would have lowered yourself like that. I mean, it was bad enough you were fucking Michael behind my back, but Lo? You're better than that," Abe said.

"You mean she *was* better than that," Eli corrected. "Now she's just tainted; funky and tainted."

"Eli, please!" Aisha snapped.

"Bitch, is that a black eye!" Eli asked in shock.

Aisha self-consciously adjusted her sunglasses.

"That nigga been beating that ass and now you seeking refuge here," Abe nodded his head knowingly.

Aisha didn't have anything to say in response.

"What happened to you, Aisha? What happened to the Aisha I fell in love with?" Hearing that perked Aisha up a little, "You were in love with me?"

"You're focusing on the wrong thing," Abe stated. "Did our break up cause you to become this irrational, foolish woman?"

Aisha shrugged her shoulders. "In a way, I guess it did."

"You shouldn't have done what you did," Eli added.

"Eli!" Eric scolded with a chuckle.

"So, what is this? Some get back shit against them?" Abe asked.

"You could say that," Aisha said. "But there's one more thing I need to tell you."

"What is that?"

"Robin."

Chapter 9

A couple of days had passed, and Robin thought she had won the battle between her and Abe. Although Lovely didn't object to Abe putting Robin out, she assured Robin they would talk and determine where their friendship stood. Robin willingly left, and of course, officially moved in Esau's condo which had somehow turned into Lorenzo's place too.

"Why did you fuck that up, Robin?" Esau asked.

"I didn't," Robin replied as she put her belongings into the walk-in closet. "Trust me, Lovely and I will patch things up, especially when she finds out the truth about Abe."

"Why didn't you just tell her now?"

Robin wore a silly smile and shrugged her shoulders. "I don't know. I just wanna fuck with Abe for a little bit. Have him at our mercy."

"You a simple bitch, you know that?" Esau sneered.

Robin scoffed and shot Esau an unbelievable look. "You sound just like your son."

"So, he's called you a simple bitch too?"

Robin cut her eyes at him and continued at her task. Lorenzo walked into the bedroom and stood in the doorway of the closet. He stared a hole into Robin. It made her uncomfortable, and she refused to look at him or even acknowledge his presence.

"Why you always fucking up shit?" Lorenzo asked in a cool manner.

Without looking at him, Robin replied, "I didn't fuck up anything. Things will still go as planned."

Lorenzo took two giant steps and was in her space so fast she didn't have enough time to guard herself. He grabbed her by the back of her neck and growled in her ear. "We were 'posed to do this shit this weekend. Stupid bitch! Now how are we gonna get Lovely by herself?"

"You don't even need me!" Robin cried out.

"You just made this shit harder for us," Lorenzo hissed as he pushed her from his grasp.

Robin shot Esau a look expecting his protection. Esau was proving to be as big of a punk as his son. Robin couldn't stand it. "I'm going to this little party, and I will talk to Lovely then."

"What party?" Esau asked.

"For the kids, it's the twins' cousin's birthday," Robin explained. "I'm gonna go ahead and tell Lovely the shit about Abe."

"She won't believe you. She sees you as a troublemaker now," Esau reasoned.

Robin sighed and looked at both men. "Trust me, I got this."

When Robin walked into the Brentwood Skate Center, she really didn't know what vibe to expect from Lovely. She knew Lovely well enough to know that she wouldn't want to cause a scene, she would act cordial. Robin just needed to speak to her alone.

Robin spotted Lovely at a table with Kam and a few other ladies. She plastered a smile on her face and headed over to the table.

"Hey ladies!"

Kam had been laughing, but her expression suddenly went blank when she looked up at Robin. "This is a kid's party and ain't nobody got time to be entertaining your messiness."

"I'm not bringing any mess," Robin said. "I just came to enjoy a good time."

Lovely smiled, "Well, glad you made it."

One of the ladies noticed the gift bag in Robin's hand. "The party room is over there. That's where everybody's been putting their gifts."

"Oh, okay," Robin almost forgot she brought a gift for the birthday girl. She stepped closer to Lovely and spoke in a lowered voice, "Do you think you and I could talk in private?"

Kam answered for Lovely, "No talking tonight boo. Like I said, this is a kid's party. No grown folks mess today."

Robin shot Kam an impatient look. "I'm speaking to Lovely."

At that moment, Bria and Grace came rushing up to Robin. Bria tugged on her. "Aunt Robin, come on and skate with us!"

"Yeah, Robin. Show us your skills." Grace egged.

Robin laughed. “What? I never said I had any skills on skates.”

“Yes you do,” Bria said as she continued to tug Robin.

Since Kam was playing bodyguard with Lovely, Robin decided she would deal with that later. Right now, there was no harm in enjoying herself for a little while.

After renting some skates, Robin joined the kids on the rink. The place was swarming with skaters of all races and ages. It was hard to tell who was attending the birthday girl’s party. It didn’t take long before she was surrounded by little giggling girls.

After thirty minutes, Grace sent the other little girls away as she continued to skate along Robin’s side.

Robin asked Grace. “Where did they go?”

“To the party room!” Grace shouted above the music.

“Oh,” Robin said. She looked ahead and standing off to the side watching her was Abe. She noticed he was accompanied by Eli. As she passed them up, she smiled in their direction and kept on around the bend with Grace. When she looked up again, she didn’t see them anymore. When she turned to say something to Grace, she discovered the young girl had left her side. Just as Robin turned her head to look for her, out of nowhere, she was knocked down. The blow knocked the wind out of her.

Robin whimpered in pain and looked up in time to see Grace skating backward wearing a mischievous grin. “You bastard!” she hollered.

Just as she was about to get up, she felt excruciating pain shoot through her hand. “Oooowww!” She looked at her hand to a big size 13 skate, smashing the life out of it.

“You need some help getting up?” Abe asked nicely while still bearing all his weight on her hand.

Robin was in so much pain she couldn’t respond. Tears came to her eyes. She wanted to curse Abe out so bad. He even had the nerve to extend a hand to help her to her feet.

Eli grabbed her by the other arm to help her up; however, her hand was still trapped under Abe’s foot.

Robin screamed in agony. “Mothafucka!”

“Oh, my bad,” Abe removed his foot. He grabbed her by the other arm.

Robin was sure her hand was broken. “What the fuck, Abe!”

Eli and Abe helped Robin to a nearby bench. “You know I know what you’ve been up to. I knew it was something about your ass I didn’t quite like.” Eli told her.

“What are you talking about?” Robin groaned as she fought back the tears. She examined her hand. It was broken. She knew it was.

Abe reached over and grabbed her damaged hand. He squeezed it as hard as he could. Robin yelled out as the pain shot all the way to her shoulder.

Abe hissed in her ear, “Shut up, bitch... shut the fuck up! You know what I’m talking about! You better be glad all I hurt this time was your hand. I’m gonna fuck more than that up if you keep fucking with me. Do you hear me?”

Robin emphatically nodded her head, pleading with her eyes for him to release her hand, but he never did as he continued to speak.

"You send this message to them two dumb mothafuckas you've been fucking. Come near my family or come with that bullshit to Lovely, I promise—I mothafuckin promise... I will hand deliver their decapitated heads to their goddamn mamas."

"Okay," Robin cried.

Eric's son Sanchez approached them, "Uncle Abe, is she okay?"

"Yeah lil' nigga. Take yo' ass on and skate," Eli snapped.

Abe squeezed her hand one last time for emphasis, "Do I make myself loud and clear?"

"Yes!" She said trying not to scream too loud.

"I suggest that you all of a sudden don't feel well and leave," Abe said dismissively as he released her hand.

Grace rolled up on them and stopped abruptly right in front of Robin, "Hey Robin."

Robin cut her eyes at Grace. She had nothing to say at this point.

"You should get that hand checked out," Eli said. "It ain't looking too good."

Kenya appreciated the turn out for Kayla's birthday party. Her daughter was having a blast. Kevin even showed up with some members from his side of the family. Kenya wanted to remain on her best behavior and not ruin Kayla's day.

It came as a surprise to her when Abe actually showed up with his wife Lovely and their twelve-year-old daughter Grace. Kenya extended the invite, but she was sure Abe didn't want anything to do with her.

As she gathered Kayla's gifts together, she noticed Lovely sitting at one of the tables, looking out into the skating rink. She was alone. Kenya thought maybe this would be a good time to have a few minutes with her. She asked her mother to continue tidying the party room.

"Hey Lovely," Kenya joined her at the table.

"Oh, hey," Lovely looked in her direction. "How's it going Kenya?"

Kenya paused and eyed Lovely suspiciously. "How did you know it was me?"

"You're the only one wearing Victoria's Secret's Strawberries & Champagne," Lovely smiled.

Kenya tried to sniff herself. "You can smell that?"

"Yeah, which reminds me. I love that coconut fragrance they have. I gotta tell Abe to grab me some," Lovely said.

"Wow. Has your nose always been that keen?" Kenya asked.

"It's gotten this way over the years," Lovely answered. "I rely on my other senses to kick in when I can't see things for myself."

Kenya nodded knowingly. "That's right, I guess."

Lovely nodded in the direction of the crowd of people skating around the rink. "Why aren't you out there enjoying yourself?"

"I don't skate. I know I'll fall on my ass," Kenya answered.

"And that's why I'm sitting over here," Lovely laughed.

"But Abe wouldn't let you fall," Kenya stated.

Lovely gave it some thought as she wore a wistful smile on her face. "No, he wouldn't."

Kenya looked around to see if she could spot Abe. When her eyes landed on him, he glanced in their direction. Kenya turned back to Lovely and cleared her throat. "So, how are things between you and Abe anyway?"

"Good. You know, Kenya," Lovely's tone switched to serious. "I've been thinking a lot about what you said to me at Kiera's repast. I even mentioned it to Abe. What exactly did you mean when you said you knew who killed my parents?"

Kenya looked back over to Abe. She found her mouth getting very dry as the nervousness settled over her. "Maybe this isn't the time to discuss this. I was wondering if we could possibly meet sometime during the week."

"That would be cool," Lovely said. "How about Monday, at Batey's... say around noon?"

"I can do that," Kenya said.

"Great," Lovely said. "I look forward to talking to you then."

"Okay. Well, I gotta get this party room in order. And I appreciate you for coming," Kenya got up.

"No problem," Lovely turned her attention back to the crowd of people.

Kenya headed back to the party room, but she could sense someone was approaching her. She looked around, and Abe was heading in her direction. “Hey, Abe. I’m glad you came out to my daughter’s party.”

“What did you say to Lovely?” Abe asked.

Kenya looked back at Lovely. “Do it look like I might have said anything out of the way to her? Look at her. She’s at peace.”

Abe looked at Lovely who was wearing the most content, pleasant expression. He looked back at Kenya. “If she tells me you said something else crazy to her, I’m coming to your house. And it ain’t gonna be for what you want it to be either.”

“Are you threatening me again?” Kenya asked smugly.

“I wouldn’t consider it a threat. It’s like fortune telling. I’m just telling you what to expect,” Abe said.

“Yeah, whatever Abe,” Kenya dismissed. When she took a step forward, she almost tripped and fell flat on her face. Fortunately, for her, the same person who tripped her was the same person that caught her.

Pretending to care about her well-being, Abe whispered to her, “Don’t make me have to show you.”

Kenya’s face furrowed in anger as she jerked away from Abe’s grasp.

“Jerk!”

Abe presented her with a sinister smile as he turned to walk away.

Chapter 10

"Daddy, how come you're not married?"

The question made Eli pause and look at Bria. "How come you ask so many questions?"

"Cause, I wanna know things. You won't know unless you ask, right?" Bria reasoned.

"Where's your brother?" Eli asked ignoring her inquisitions.

"He's coming. But Daddy," Bria snatched her Hello Kitty lunchbag from the counter and followed Eli out the kitchen.

"Bryce! C'mon before you get left!" Eli called out. He turned back around only to bump into Bria.

She giggled. "But why you live in this big house with no wife?"

"What do you know about a wife?" Eli asked.

Bryce came running around the corner, letting his hands trail along the glass walls. Eli cringed at the sound it made knowing it was leaving behind streaks. He snapped.

"Boy, what have I told you about touching the glass?"

"Oops," Bryce said. "Sorry, Eli—I mean Dad."

"I told you; it's okay if you call me Eli. I know it'll take some time to get used to," Eli said.

"Mama used to call a lot of men our daddy," Bria said.

Eli looked at her blankly. "I didn't need to know that."

Bria wouldn't let up as she followed Eli and Bryce to the garage. "But Daddy... If you had a wife, she could help take care of us."

"You don't think I do a sufficient job?" Eli asked.

Bria climbed into her usual spot in the second-row seating in Eli's SUV. Bryce took his place beside her. "You do an okay job, Daddy," she said.

Bryce added, "If you had a wife, then maybe she could fetch your sodas from the kitchen instead of using us as your slaves."

That tickled Eli. Having kids did come in handy when it came to him enjoying the pleasures of being lazy. Bria and Bryce were his two tiny servants.

Eli relented just to shut Bria up. "Okay, okay lil' girl. I'll consider finding a wife."

Bria sat back in her seat as if her purpose for the day had been served.

As soon as Eli dropped the kids off at school, he called the one person that had been on his mind since Bria started with the questions that morning.

Kris answered. "Hello?"

"Good morning," Eli greeted.

The smile came through the phone as she spoke, "Hey, I was just thinking about you."

"I hope it was about something good."

"It was. It always is."

"So when are you coming?" Eli asked.

"I don't know."

"What do you mean you don't know? I thought we talked about this, Kris."

"We did, but..." her voice trailed.

"But what?"

"If I come, I won't be coming alone," Kris blurted out.

"Who you tryna bring with you? I ain't taking care of no grown ass people," Eli stated.

Kris laughed. "It ain't like that. It's a kid."

"A kid? Like your niece or nephew?"

Kris was hesitant. "It's a girl, and not my niece or nephew. It's someone that relies on me to take care of her."

"A girl? How old is she?" he asked.

"Oh, she's a little kid."

Eli gave it some thought. "Okay. Bring her. I have more than enough room."

"Are you sure?"

"Kris, I want us to have something together. And it's not gonna work with you in North Carolina, and I'm over here in Tennessee."

Kris remained quiet.

"When I told you I loved you the last time you were here, I meant it. And I'm tired of not having someone special in my life. I mean, I have kids now, but they're a different kind of special... Shit. Besides, Bria just questioned me this morning about why I don't have a wife."

Kris chuckled. "She did, for real?"

"Yeah, I guess to her it doesn't seem normal that I don't live like she sees Abe living."

"So, me and Avani... we come to live with you... then what?"

"What do you mean?" he asked.

"We just live there?"

"Avani? That's the child's name? Who is this child? Why are you taking care of another person's child?" Eli wanted to know.

"Eli, don't worry about that. Just know I'm not coming if she can't come."

"Is the mama some trifling crack head whore that left her child on you? Turn that child over to the state, Kris."

Kris was laughing. "Eli, you are a mess. I'm on my way to work. Can I call you later?"

"Yeah, you can call me back. You better call me back," Eli teased.

"Okay, I will." Kris hung up.

Eli frowned. He called her back.

"What Eli?" She sang into the phone.

"Is there something you forgot to tell me?"

"What?"

"Those three words."

"Oh! You know I love you, silly."

Eli smiled. "I love you too. Have a great day at work baby." With that, he was satisfied enough to end the call.

Lovely sat patiently as she waited for her lunch date to accompany her. A part of her was anxious to know what information Kenya had to share. However, another part of her was afraid to know anything.

"I think this bad idea," Lulu said.

"We're just having lunch, Lulu," Lovely reasoned.

"Abe not know we're here. He found out, he fire me."

Lovely chuckled. "Abe ain't firing nobody."

Lulu's eyes widen. "He kick out Robin! You say nothing."

"That was different," Lovely explained. "Let's just enjoy our lunch, okay."

"What can ex-girl have to say to you? Abe move on, he with you now. He marry you. You have baby. You have ring. You have last name."

"She does not want to talk to me about Abe," Lovely said. "It's about my parents."

"She knew your parents?" Lulu asked.

"No, she said she might know who killed them."

Lulu let out a sound that clearly signified her skepticism. She laughed. "She know nothing, she pulling your leg."

"Well, I'm about to find out, today," Lovely took a sip of the lemonade before her.

"Lovely, she tells you, then what?" Lulu questioned.

"Then, I know."

"But life is good, Lovely. *Haima non non.*"

Lovely looked at Lulu as if she could see her. "What did you just say?"

"I said, *'let sleeping dogs lie.'* You understand, Lovely?"

Lovely broke out into one of her famous goofy grins. "Can you say that again in Laotian?"

"No Lovely," Lulu said waving her off. "I say to you what's the point. Leave it alone. What will you get from it? No need to open sensitive matter for you, family, Abe, and the baby you carry."

Lovely gasped. No one knew she was pregnant except Abe.

"How do you know?"

Lulu sat back and smiled. "I know."

"But how?"

Lulu's attention turned to Kenya walking through the front entrance of the restaurant. She patted Lovely's hand tenderly. "I just know... Abe ex here now. I go to ladies' room."

Before Lovely could object, the spot that Lulu once sat in across from her was immediately occupied by Kenya. Lovely smiled, "Ah! Pear Glace, I like that one too."

"You really know your smells, huh?" Kenya made herself comfortable.

"I do. So, do you want to order something to eat?"

"Sure. I guess we can get that out of the way."

The two ladies made small talk as they waited for their food to arrive. The more she sat there, the more Lovely realized she didn't want to know. She didn't want to delve into that part of her life that she had perfectly secured away. Abe and Lulu were right. *Why would she want to disrupt the lives of her family by unleashing the darkness of the past?*

Lovely finally said to Kenya, "I don't want to know anymore Kenya. So, whatever you know, just take it to your grave."

Kenya stared back at the lovely woman before her and felt somewhat relieved. The more she sat with Lovely, the more difficult she found this situation.

"I got too many happy things going on in my life to entertain that. I don't wanna lose how I feel now," Lovely sat back and rubbed her stomach. "The baby and I really don't need the stress."

Kenya stared at Lovely's stomach, noticing its roundness for the first time. "You're pregnant?"

Lovely smiled. "I am. No one knows except you and ol' Lulu here."

"Wow. You and Abe are wasting no time, huh? How old is the other baby?"

"AJ is only three months old."

Kenya smiled, "Well, congratulations."

"Thanks."

Kenya sighed and let her shoulders drop. She smiled thoughtfully. "You know what Lovely, at first I was a little jealous of you. I really wanted to rekindle things with Abe. But he's different now. I'm different. That old love we once had wouldn't be the same if we tried it today."

"So, are you trying to say you were going to take my man?" Lovely asked playfully.

"Yeah, but Abe wasn't having it anyway. He really, truly loves you. What you two have is something beautiful. It's something I wouldn't mind having with someone one day," Kenya said with thought. "But you... I don't think a better woman out there could be more perfect for Abe than you."

Lovely blushed. "Well, thank you Kenya. That means a lot."

"At this point, I'm not sure if I got all of the facts together anyway. No need in spreading information if you don't know how factual it is," Kenya said.

"You're absolutely right," Lovely agreed.

"I appreciate this little lunch date," Kenya said.

"I do too. Talking with you has been nice," Lovely said.

Lulu rolled her eyes. "Can you quit with mushy talk. Eat! Hurry. Need to see Young and Restless."

Chapter 11

Robin downed the remainder of her vodka to chase the two pain pills she had taken. She was vexed. Her mind was going a mile a minute. She looked at her hand. It was protected in hardened plaster. She couldn't believe that mothafucka had actually broken her hand. The emergency room doctors referred her to follow up with an orthopedic surgeon because her fractures show evidence that more than one metacarpal had been damaged. They said she would likely need surgery. Robin didn't have time to think about surgery though. She would deal with that once she and Esau were settled into their new life.

For the time being, she had some business to take care of. She dialed Lovely's phone number and waited, only to be sent to voicemail. Robin's drunken state only contributed to her aggravation and frustration.

"Answer the phone you blind bitch!"

"Robin, calm your ass down," Esau told her.

"No. She needs to answer the phone, so I can tell her about her sorry ass husband," Robin slurred. "Who does that, Esau? That bastard broke my hand!"

"Don't worry baby, we'll get him for everything he's done," Esau said with a slight smile.

"This shit isn't funny Esau!" Robin yelled. She looked at her phone as if an idea suddenly entered her mind. "Oh, I'll call that bratty little bitch Grace."

"Why would you call her?" Esau asked.

Robin dialed the number as she spoke, "So she can give the phone to her mama... Hello... Grace!"

"This is not Grace. Who is this?" Lovely asked.

"Lovely?"

"Robin? Did you mean to call Grace?"

"I did call Grace. I wanted her to give the phone to you. You weren't answering your phone."

Lovely chuckled. "This is your first time calling my phone. You must have been dialing the wrong number. Besides, Grace doesn't even have a phone. Are you okay? You sound a little off."

Robin straightened her posture. "I'm fine, except for the fact that your husband broke my hand the other day."

"Your hand is broken? What do you mean?"

"Abe broke my mothafuckin hand! I gotta get surgery and everything!"

Lovely remained calm and concerned. "When did this happen? Are you sure Abe did that?"

"Yes, I'm sure. Your husband is evil. That's why he got rid of me. I'm not a liar, Lovely. Listen to me!"

"I'm listening," Lovely assured her.

Robin paused to listen to the loud chatter and laughter going on in Lovely's background. She whispered, "Lovely, leave the house. Abe is gonna get you."

Lovely laughed. "What? You're not making any sense."

"Go somewhere far away from everybody. I gotta tell you something very, very important."

Robin could hear the noise in the background fade. It meant Lovely had moved into another room. "Lovely?"

"I'm still listening. You know it's Monday, and everybody's over. They're kind of loud."

"Who's everybody?"

"You know, the usual."

Robin sighed as if what she was about to say would be so difficult. "Listen, Lovely—"

"What happened between you and Abe?" Lovely cut her off. "Do we need to handle the medical bill for your hand?"

"No. I don't give a damn about that! I want us to be friends like we used to be. But Abe won't let us. You know why he won't let us? Cause that mothafucka keeping secrets. And I know about 'em!"

"What secrets, Robin? Please start making sense."

"Okay. The reason Abe got rid of me was because I told him I was gonna tell you the whole truth about him."

"But Robin, you've already tried to cause troubles between me and Abe by telling me he tried to come on to you. What makes you think that—"

"Lovely! Listen! Abe killed your parents!"

There was silence.

Robin started sobbing. "I've wanted to tell you ever since I found out. He did it. He was the one—him, Eric, and his cousin Lorenzo. Why do you think Abe has a problem with Lorenzo coming around? Lorenzo wants to tell you! They killed your parents. And one of them raped you... And they shot you. It was them."

Lovely snapped. "This is not funny, Robin! I know you tend to be jealous but to go this far! Don't call me ever again with this mess!"

"Lovely, Lovely... No! I'm telling you the truth. Think about it; his past. Ask him where he got so much money from at such a young age. It was the money he took from your daddy. Just ask him. He won't be able to deny it. You gotta believe me. Why would he go to this extreme to get rid of me and break my fuckin hand, Lovely! He knows that I know. And I'm exposing him!"

"Bye Robin," Lovely whispered before hanging up.

Robin looked at her phone, and then at Esau who had been eagerly listening. A wide smile crept across Robin's face. "The game has just begun!"

Lovely's heart was racing a mile a minute. Her hands suddenly became clammy. Her breathing hitched. She felt faint. She thought she was on the verge of hyperventilating.

This was absurd. The things Robin said were ridiculous. No way. Lovely tried to dismiss them. However, the whole scene days ago between Abe and Robin replayed in Lovely's mind.

"I'm very serious. You better realize who the fuck you fucking with," Abe threatened.

"Abe, just go!"

"You see how violent he is?" Robin asked. "I'm surprised he doesn't go around killing people's parents and shit of that nature."

"Abe, stop it! Just go, leave!"

Lovely didn't want to believe that Robin could be telling the truth. But even she had to admit Abe's behavior had been odd.

Then it hit Lovely like a ton of bricks; the reason Lorenzo's voice creeped her out. It was the same raspy voice that was in her ear as she was violently raped. A voice she worked so hard to clear from her mind. There was also a familiarity to Eric's voice that she never wanted to acknowledge. No! Even Abe—his eyes!

"Oh Jesus," Lovely managed as she doubled over in anguish. "No, no, no... No!"

Lovely tried to blink back the tears, but it was inevitable. They blurred her already impaired vision even more, but it didn't stop her from rushing through the house. She found her way downstairs where mostly everyone was.

It was Monday night. The big oversized screen displayed a football game between New England Patriots and Kansas City Chiefs. Lovely knew this because the men had been going back and forward about the game and talking stats. The atmosphere was rambunctious as it always was on these nights. It was one of the joys of the week that Lovely looked forward to. She always loved it when her family gathered in one place. There was always a lot of love and laughter exchanged; memories made.

As she neared the sitting area of the huge man cave, Lovely tried to remember what color shirt Abe was wearing. Her mind was so rattled she couldn't focus.

"Abe," she called out.

"Yeah," he said absently, not really looking in her direction.

Luciano was the first to take notice of Lovely's distressed state. From where he was sitting, Luciano asked, "Is everything okay, Lovely?"

The concern in Luciano's voice made everyone glance in Lovely's direction. Abe actually did a double take. Worry etched across his face as he immediately rose from the sofa to be at her side.

Oh my God, Lovely thought. He's coming towards me. *What do I say? How should I feel?* In those seconds, Lovely wasn't sure of how she should feel. She knew she felt sick. She held her hand out to stop him from coming any closer.

Abe looked at Lovely's outstretched arm in confusion.

"Baby, what's wrong?"

"Robin just called me," Lovely said calmly.

Everyone got quiet to listen to what Lovely was saying. The television still played noisily.

"What did she have to say now?" Abe asked.

"Why did you break her hand, Abe?" Lovely asked.

"She told you that?" Abe tried to maintain an innocent stance although he could tell from the look on Lovely's face this was about more than Robin's broken hand.

"She told me that and some other things." She continued to talk in a low, even, and calm manner, but the tears welling in her eyelids were in contrast.

Luciano sensed there was something occurring between Abe and Lovely, but he didn't know what. He was curious and concerned enough to get up.

"Lovely, what's going on?"

Ignoring Luciano, whom she allowed to come near her, Lovely asked Abe, "Did you kill my parents?"

The lump that formed in his throat was hard for him to swallow. He couldn't open his mouth to speak. At this point, he didn't know if he should lie or go ahead and admit to the truth.

Lovely repeated her question, but with more emotion. "Did you, Eric and Lorenzo kill my parents?"

Luciano looked from Lovely to Abe. "What is she talking about?"

"Who told you that shit?" Eric asked.

"Lovely—" Abe was saying but was cut off by her motioning for him to be quiet.

"Abe, just tell me the truth," Lovely said firmly.

"Wait a minute, Lovely," Luciano said trying to lighten the situation. "Don't you think that's a silly accusation? Abe couldn't have possibly..." Luciano's words trailed as his eyes met Abe's. If Abe was innocent, he wasn't doing a good job of saying it with his eyes, "Abe?"

Abe opened his mouth to speak, but when nothing came out, Lovely went into a rage. That was the only answer she needed. She attacked him. Abe had to grab her by her wrists to restrain her. He tried to soothe her.

"Lovely, baby, listen. Just listen to me."

Lovely continued to fight. "Let go of me! You have no right to touch me! Ever!... Let me go!"

Luciano grabbed Lovely by her waist and pulled her away. Cesar came to Lovely's side.

"Lovely, calm down."

"Abe, is this true?" Luciano asked.

"No, it's not," Eric answered.

"They killed my parents!" Lovely screamed as Cesar tried to hold her back. "They did it, and this sick fuck had the nerve to marry me... and have a child with me. And... Oh, God... I'm pregnant now with another one of your babies, why Abe?"

"Lovely, let me explain," Abe finally said.

"Don't," Eric said to Abe. He shook his head emphatically hoping Abe would just keep his mouth closed.

"Get outta my house!" Lovely yelled, "Both of you!"

"Let's talk about this, Lovely," Abe said.

"Nothing to talk about," Lovely cried. Suddenly, she could see him. It was a brief second, but she saw one of the home invaders. It was Abe. Everything matched—his height, his complexion, his voice, and his eyes. Lovely remembered the person had a set of the evilest blue eyes. *How could blue eyes look like they were filled with so much fire?* Lovely started crying uncontrollably as she tried to get the words out, "I know... I know... what you look like... It was you... you were there, oh God!"

Abe wanted to hold her and take the hurt away. He couldn't stand to see Lovely so overcome with emotion. She always managed to keep herself together. It tore at his heart to hear her crying with so much pain. "Baby, I'm sorry."

"You damn right! Only somebody evil could do what you've done, Abe!" Lovely yelled. She composed herself enough to snidely add, "Or, should I call you Abaddon?"

That really hit Abe hard.

Lovely continued. "Your mama was right for naming you that. You ain't nothing but Satan himself."

"You don't mean that, Lovely," Abe said.

Lovely was angry. "Oh yes, I do! I want a divorce, and I never want you around my children or me again."

"But that's not who I am anymore. You know that's not who I am anymore. If I could take all of it back, I would. Baby, please forgive me." Abe's eyelids began to burn as they welled with tears. He took a step toward her, but she was guarded by Cesar. Abe pleaded, "Lovely, please, listen to me."

"What can you say, Abe?" Lovely cried.

She was right. What could he say?

"I don't know, but I don't want to leave. I want you to forgive me," he pled desperately. "I love you so much and I never—"

"Never wanted me to find out?" Lovely completed his sentence.

"No," he whispered. "You weren't supposed to."

"How long have you known? When we first met? When we first became intimate? When we got married? After we had AJ; how long?"

"Before we got married," Abe answered.

From a very low place, Lovely said, "Get out. Get out of my house and out of my life."

"Lovely, weren't you always the one that told me my past didn't determine who I was today? You always told me to—"

She interrupted him, "That went out the window when it was my parents that you killed!"

"So, you did do it?" Luciano asked in disbelief.

Abe looked at Cesar and Antino. Neither one of them displayed any guilt. When Abe shifted his eyes back to Luciano, he wasn't expecting the punch the older man connected with his jaw.

"You son of a bitch, you killed my best friend!" Luciano bellowed.

This time it was both Cesar and Antino trying to hold Luciano back as everyone else in the room looked on in horror.

That sick feeling returned to Lovely. It was too much to stomach; too much to accept all at once. The room started spinning, and everyone's voices started to blend.

She managed to whisper his name. "Abe..."

Then she heard someone yell. "Catch her!" Before she hit the floor.

Chapter 12

It took Eli thirty minutes to convince his brother to go home with him. There was absolutely nothing Abe could say to persuade Luciano or Lovely into letting him remain at the house. Luciano really wanted to kick Abe's ass. Eli couldn't blame him though. *Did Abe really expect to get away with what he did without any repercussions?*

Eli checked in on his brother before retiring to bed himself. He stood in the doorway to the bedroom that would become Abe's new resting place. Abe should have been asleep, but he stood by the sliding glass doors that exited to the private terrace outside. The moon cascaded a light right outside of the room, but it shone on nothing spectacular. Abe just stared out into nothingness.

"Are you okay, Abe?" Eli asked.

"Maybe," Abe murmured.

Maybe, what kind of answer was that? Eli stepped further into the room. "Are you gonna stand there and stare outside all night?"

"Maybe."

"Abe?"

"Hmm?"

Eli knew his brother was out of it. He listened to Abe for the past two hours, crying and declaring how much he loved Lovely, Grace and AJ. "You should lie down for a while."

"I can't," Abe looked back at Eli. "I think I need to go back home."

"Home? You're talking about that big ol' house you used to live in with Lovely? Yeah, that's not your home anymore. Didn't you hear Lovely?"

"Lovely isn't thinking clearly right now. She's just upset," Abe reasoned.

Eli couldn't believe his brother had just said that. "Are you thinking clearly right now? There's no way Lovely would want you back anytime soon. She hates you."

"No she doesn't," Abe said. "Lovely doesn't know how to hate people."

"She was throwing a whole bunch of hate your way tonight," Eli pointed out.

"Out of anger," he said.

Eli threw his hands up with a perplexed expression. "What the fuck Abe? Are you experiencing a delusional episode? Lovely will be reminded that she hates your guts every time she comes near you."

"Wow, Eli. Thanks for making me feel better about the whole situation," Abe said sarcastically.

Eli was apologetic. "I'm sorry. I guess that isn't helping any."

"I fucked up," Abe said thoughtfully.

"Uh... yeah," Eli said as he sat down on the edge of the bed.

"No, I mean I fucked up by trying to play the good guy."

"Huh?"

"I should have handled this the old way."

"I'm missing something. The old way is what got you in this situation in the first place."

"I'm saying Eli. I should have just killed all them mothafuckas at first."

"So you just wanna kill everybody?" Eli asked.

"Ain't that what I said?"

Eli scratched his head. "I think I need to go to bed."

Abe looked at Eli, and a small smile crept across his face. "How far does your memory go back?"

"I don't know. Why?"

"Do you remember Grandmama?" Abe asked.

Eli replied, "A little bit."

"Every summer she would have all of the grandkids at her house. We all were inseparable the entire summer and when it was time for school to start, all of y'all would leave, and I'd be the only one left behind. You would always cry when Mama and Esau came to get you and Ike."

"I do remember Grandmama's big yellow house. And them damn Beenie Weenies she used to feed our asses. What was up with that? Ike used to gag cause he hated any kind of beans," Eli said with a laugh.

"And spam," Abe added.

"I remember that damn station wagon she used to pile us all in too," Eli said.

"You know half them kids weren't even related to us?"

"Damn, I thought we had a gang of cousins," Eli replied.

"Remember when we used to run away from Lil' Joe, because he sucked his fingers, and whoever he touched with those fingers was destined to die a horrible death."

Eli burst into laughter. "Didn't nobody wanna get touched by them wet, soggy, stinky fingers."

"If you run into him today he'll swear he didn't suck on his fingers."

"I bet that nigga still do in his sleep," Eli said. He eyed Abe suspiciously. He asked, "Where did all of that come from?"

"I was just remembering a time when I thought life was supposed to be easy," Abe said. His expression saddened as he began to cry. "I wished Grandmama stayed a little longer. I wish she was here to tell me everything will be all right."

Tears welled up in Eli's eyes. He couldn't stand to see his brother hurting. Abe represented so much strength to him that to witness him in such a state was devastating. "I know I'm not Grandmama, but I can assure you that everything will be alright. So, could you please stop crying, please?" Eli said.

"Eli, I need Lovely in my life," Abe said desperately.

"I know," Eli responded soothingly. "Just give her some space so she can sort all this out." Even if it wasn't realistic, Eli wanted Abe to believe that everything would work out.

Lovely's heart was heavy. It literally felt like it added more weight to her physical being. She was glad the doctor told her to take it easy and get some rest. She didn't want to get out of bed anyway.

No matter how much she wanted not to, she could only think of Abe. At one point, she couldn't imagine her life without that man. He acted like he loved every fiber of her being. He loved her down to the dirt under her nails. *But could his love for her have been out of guilt this whole time? Furthermore, if Abe did these things, could she forgive him and look past it all?*

"What do you mean, if?" She asked herself out loud. "He did it!"

"Did what?" Grace asked as she plopped on the bed beside Lovely. "Mama, are you talking to yourself again?"

"Yeah, a little," Lovely propped herself up on her side.

"Where's Abe?" Grace asked.

"Not here," Lovely was thankful the kids hadn't been downstairs to witness her outburst the night before.

"Are you and Abe fighting?"

"Why do you ask that?"

"Well, he wasn't here last night before I went to bed. He wasn't here this morning before I went to school, and he's not here now. So, my best guess is that you two are fighting."

"No, we're not fighting," Lovely lied. "He just got some major business to handle."

"Oh. Well, when he gets here, tell him I need to see him," Grace gave Lovely a peck on the cheek. "I got homework to do, so, see ya!"

Lovely watched Grace skip out the room. Her mind wandered to AJ. She hadn't been much of a good mother all day. She left him in the care of Aunt Livy and Lulu. She had to ask herself if her reasoning for being neglectful was in any way connected to her disappointment in his father. She missed AJ, and it made her heart smile just thinking about him. She needed to hold her baby and spend some time with him.

There was a knock on the door.

Lovely looked toward her doorway. "Who goes there?"

"It's me!" Robin said. She walked over and sat down beside Lovely on the edge of the bed. "I just wanted to come by and check on you."

"Thanks," Lovely said.

"So, I heard what happened. How are you handling all of this?" Robin asked with concern.

"I don't even know, Robin. I mean, one minute I was the happiest woman on earth, and the next minute, all of my happiness was just snatched right from me."

"I'm sorry. I know I'm to blame for it."

"Oh no, don't apologize. You did nothing wrong. I should have been listening to you all along. You were just being a friend, and I guess I was just too in love to pay attention to everything. If anything, I should say I'm sorry."

"But it wasn't to upset you in any way. And I surely didn't intend to rob you of your joy."

"You're fine. Abe is the culprit in all of this. How's your hand?"

Robin lifted her casted arm for Lovely to feel. "It's alright for now. They think I might need surgery."

"Just let me know, and I'll be more than happy to pay for the cost. It's the least I can do."

Robin looked at Lovely's swollen red eyes. It was evident she'd been crying for some time. "Why don't we go out and get some fresh air? Let's go to the mall or something. You need to get out the house. You don't need to wallow in your sorrows."

"Thanks for the offer but I really do have to pass. I just need some time to recuperate and be to myself for a little while. But as soon as I'm up for it, we can have a girls' day out. I promise."

Robin was somewhat disappointed. "That's cool. It's whenever."

"Where are you staying? You know you're welcomed to come back here."

"Oh, I'm staying at this nice little condo downtown. And I love it. It has really nice views from every room. So, I'm good on that."

Lovely smiled with remorse heavy on her shoulders. "I really am sorry, Robin. I mean, I knew something wasn't right when you told me he broke your hand."

"You don't have to keep being sorry. We can just pick up where we left off as if nothing happened."

"I know. I just feel really terrible."

"So, what did Lu say about all of this?" Robin asked.

"Lu is so devastated and disappointed. It really hurt him. I mean, he just discovered Abe was his son; the son who killed his best friend."

"Yeah, that's gotta suck," Robin said sympathetically. She looked at Lovely with suspicion. "But how are you really doing?"

"I'm okay, I guess," Lovely said in a dispirited manner.

"Where do you and Abe stand now?"

Lovely shrugged. "I don't know."

Robin frowned. "What do you mean you don't know? Abe is a monster. No thought needs to be given when it comes to him."

Lovely thought it over. Sadness consumed her instantly as she realized the words Robin said were true. "You're absolutely right. But I don't know what we're going to do moving forward. I mean, we have a child together. And technically, he's Grace's father too."

"Do you really think someone like Abe should be around kids like that? I mean, what kind of influence do you think he would have over them? Can you even trust him?"

"Abe loves our kids," Lovely argued.

Sensing Lovely's defensiveness, Robin said, "Okay, whatever. I just hope he doesn't disappoint you yet again."

"I won't be dealing with Abe one on one anymore," Lovely mumbled. She sighed heavily with despair. "This is just one big crazy mess."

Robin tried to suppress the smile threatening to spread across her face. "Well, I'm here when you need me. Just call."

Lovely nodded.

Robin leaned down to give Lovely a hug before leaving. As she exited Lovely's bedroom, she bumped into Lulu who was giving her the evil eye. Robin smirked, “And how are you, Lulu?”

Lulu cut her eyes at Robin, shook her head in pity, and continued to Lovely’s bedroom.

Robin laughed to herself. “I’m gonna get rid of that bitch too.”

Chapter 13

Three days later, Lovely found herself in a state of shock as she left her doctor's office. This was the first visit she had ever gone to without Abe. She knew he would have been ecstatic if he had heard what Dr. Bradshaw just informed her.

Twins; that's what Dr. Bradshaw suspected. He wasn't one-hundred percent sure; therefore, he needed to send Lovely to get another ultrasound to confirm that she was pregnant with multiples. When he was listening for the baby's heartbeat, there was an off-rhythm beat going on that lead him to believe there was more than one. Along with the size she was measuring, Dr. Bradshaw was positive Lovely was carrying twins.

While Lulu drove, Lovely decided to place a phone call. Luciano answered on the second ring, "*Ciao mio caro*!"

Lovely smiled. "Well, don't you sound in better spirits."

"It's getting better," Luciano said. "How about you? How have you been feeling?"

"About the same, I just left Dr. Bradshaw's and that visit really didn't help matters any."

"Why not, is everything okay?"

"Everything is fine. He just thinks there may be two this time."

Luciano exclaimed excitedly. "What!"

"Yeah," Lovely sighed.

"That's great Lovely. That's two more grandbabies for me."

"I guess," her tone wasn't very convincing. "Have you spoken to your son?"

"Actually, I have. We talked business."

"How could you even continue to do business with him?" Lovely asked in disbelief.

"He's a part of BevyCo Lovely," Luciano explained. He was hesitant as he continued, "And he's my son."

"Really Lu?" Lovely couldn't believe any of this. Luciano was supposed to be just as upset as she was.

"It's not anything I would expect you to understand. I'm still upset that my son had any involvement in all of that. And maybe if he wasn't my son, Abe would be dealt with accordingly."

Lovely's lips grew tight the angrier she became. No one seemed to have any regards to the emotional turmoil she was going through.

"I can't believe this. So, the two of you have kissed and made up?"

"I'm not saying that. There's definitely some tension there that he and I need to clear. It's just that I'm not really ready to have that discussion."

As angry as Lovely wanted to be she could understand Luciano's position. He was torn between his newfound love for a son he never knew he had and the loyalty he had to a dear friend. At times, for brief seconds of uncertainty, Lovely wrestled with the thought of once being in love with the father of her child who was also her husband, and the idea that her husband was responsible for the death of her parents. It was so heart wrenching; almost unbearable.

Lovely needed to get away. She needed some serious alone time, so she could think clearly. "Well, Luciano, I'm sure I'll understand once the dust settles. Right now, I just can't wrap my mind around any of this. In fact, I think I'll leave for a couple of days; take a mini vacation."

"That's probably what you need anyway. Do you need me to make arrangements for you?"

"No, because I don't even know where I'm going," Lovely chuckled.

"Why don't you accompany Cesar to Miami this weekend? He leaves out tonight."

A smile spread across Lovely's face. "That's a good idea!"

Why? That was the question Abe needed an answer to. *Why would Cesar want Lovely's father dead? Why would Antino go along with it knowing that Dharmesh was his brother's best friend?* It didn't make sense to Abe. *Antino was the main one always telling Abe that people weren't who they appear to be, but who was he?* Something wasn't adding up.

"You alright over there?" Eric asked interrupting Abe's thoughts.

Abe shifted his eyes to his friend and nodded.

"You're sure?" Eli asked. He was sitting next to Abe at one of the tables in the VIP section of Southern Wild.

"You look like shit," Eric joked.

"Fuck you," Abe mumbled.

The music was loud, but Abe was sure Eric read his lips. Being at the club was supposed to be a distraction for him, but all he could think about was this entire dilemma. His mind was constantly on how he could win Lovely back. She had nothing to do with him. Every time he called, she sent him straight to voicemail. He was sure she didn't listen to any of the messages he left either.

"Naw, seriously man," Eric said. "You look like you ain't been sleeping."

"I'm good," Abe said.

Eric's attention turned to a female passing by. She gave them seductive glances with her eyes lingering longer on Abe. "You got bitches checking you out. Maybe that'll get your mind off things." Eric told him.

Abe didn't even bother looking in the direction Eric was looking. "That's the last thing I need to be doing."

"Are you suggesting that my brother cheat on his wife?" Eli asked.

"Hell, it ain't no worse than the shit he's already done," Eric reasoned. "Lovely, ain't about to take his ass back; no time soon anyway."

"Shut the fuck up, Eric," Abe warned. He shot his friend a daring look. Abe wasn't trying to hear Eric's nonsense.

Eric threw his hands up in surrender. "Hey, I'm just tryna keep it real with you, so your expectations ain't so mothafuckin high."

"I'm not worried about that shit you talking about," Abe said. "I'm getting my family back; period."

"Lovely... don't want your ass. Accept it," Eric said.

"Like I said—" Abe was saying before he got totally annoyed and frustrated with Eric. "What the fuck is wrong you? Why you keep saying shit like that?"

Eli shifted in his seat with uneasiness. If Eric kept it up, Eli knew Abe was going to knock a couple of knots upside Eric's head.

"I'm just being one hunit with you. Stop moping over this shit," Eric said.

Eli cleared his throat to intervene. "Eric, just leave it alone."

"I'll leave it alone," Eric said. He was focused on someone in the distance. He nodded in their direction. "But you still gotta deal with that mothafucka right there."

Abe and Eli turned to look in the direction Eric was looking. Abe's face immediately expressed his disdain for the person heading their way.

Lorenzo was accompanied by two goons on each side of him. Abe wasn't familiar with who they were.

"You know them, Eric?"

"Hell naw."

Lorenzo was wearing one of his infamous devilish smirks. "What's up cuzzo!"

Abe casually turned his back to Lorenzo. He wasn't in the mood to deal with Lorenzo's stupidity.

Lorenzo lowered his head in between Abe and Eli to say to Abe, “We need to discuss some shit, Cuz.”

Abe didn’t reply. Lorenzo turned to Eli. “Can you move over so I can talk to Abe real quick?”

Eli’s face screwed up with disgust. He covered his nose. “Why did you just assault me like that?”

Lorenzo was confused, “What the fuck? Man, move your ass over.”

“Naw, for real! Mothafucka, yo’ breath smell like you been eating some expired pussy. That shit was spoilt!” Eli exclaimed.

Lorenzo scoffed with a slight laugh, “Eating pussy, huh? What would you know about that, ol’ gay ass mothafucka? Move the fuck over.”

“I’ll move!” Eli said as he moved to the next chair. “Just don’t say nothing to me again before I have you arrested for assault!”

As bad of a mood Abe was in, he couldn’t help but chuckle just a little at his brother’s silly antics.

Lorenzo sat down beside Abe. He nodded his acknowledgment towards Eric before speaking to Abe. “So, what’s up?”

“What’s up?” Abe countered.

“You know what I’m asking about,” Lorenzo said.

“I can’t help you,” Abe said shaking his head. “Lovely already knows, so this blackmailing shit ain’t working anymore.”

Lorenzo glanced at Eric, and then at the two guys that he came with. He looked back at Abe with a wicked grin. "So she knows?"

Abe nodded.

"Everything?" Lorenzo asked.

Abe responded with a cold stare into Lorenzo's eyes.

"Well, it looks like I'm gonna have to get my money a different way," Lorenzo said as he got up.

"What the fuck that mean?" Abe stood up ready to pounce on Lorenzo.

Eric jumped up ready to restrain Abe. "Man, fuck that nigga," he said. "You got other shit to worry about."

"Nothing cuz, y'all take it easy," Lorenzo said cordially before walking away without a care with the two goons.

Eli asked Abe, "How could you let him talk to you like that? Goddamn!"

Abe just shook his head as his phone began to vibrate. He looked down at the screen, and it was a call from home.

"Hello?"

"I don't know what's going on, but Mama is leaving," Grace said. She sounded worried.

"What do you mean she's leaving?" Abe got up to head to an area that was less noisy.

"She had me to pack her some clothes for the weekend. What's going on between you two? How come you haven't been home?" Grace wanted to know.

"Nothing is going on that you need to be concerned about," Abe explained as gentle as he could. "Where's she going? Is she taking AJ with her?"

"No. And Mama don't like leaving AJ behind, so something isn't right," Grace said.

Panic began to settle over Abe. *Where could Lovely be going?*

"Has she left already?"

"Uncle Cesar just came to pick her up. She's going somewhere with him."

"Okay. Let me call you back?" Abe said as he headed back to the table.

"Okay," Grace ended the call.

Abe told Eric he had to leave. Eli didn't hesitate to follow behind his brother.

"What's going on Abe?" he asked once they got outside to the private parking area.

"Lovely is about to leave with Cesar. And I can't let that happen."

Lovely was somewhat disappointed when Cesar informed her that they wouldn't be leaving until first thing in the morning. She was ready to get away. She was beginning to think Cesar had something else up his sleeve.

"Are you okay, Lovely?" Cesar asked.

Lovely nodded. It was hard to make out his body due to the dim lighting in his condo. She was beginning to think that leaving might not be such a good idea. She was already missing AJ and Grace.

"You look a little down," Cesar said as he sat down beside her on the sofa.

"I'm just missing my babies," Lovely said softly.

"Already?"

Lovely chuckled, "Yeah. I hope AJ is fine without me."

"He'll be fine. He's in good hands. Aunt Livy and Lulu won't let anything happen to him," Cesar assured her.

"Yeah, I know."

Cesar admired the girliness in Lovely that she had yet to grow out of. She was still the same fresh face girl from years ago. It was her eyes and her smile. Her eyes always twinkled with elation, and her smile always brightened a room.

"So, how have you been feeling lately?" Cesar asked.

Lovely gave a listless half shrug. "I don't know."

"Have you decided where you and Abe will go from here?"

She shook her head. "A part of me wants a divorce. I want to be as far from him as possible. I don't want him nowhere near me and the kids. Then, another part of me doesn't want to accept any of this and continue to live as if nothing ever happened."

"Would you like to know my opinion on the matter?" Cesar asked.

"Not really, but go ahead."

"I say divorce his ass. Abe has got to be dealt with," Cesar said in a serious tone.

Lovely was taken aback. “Dealt with; like how?”

“Do you think your people will let him live after this? Trust me, they’re coming for him.”

“Who told them?” Lovely asked frantically.

Noticing her composure changed, Cesar asked, “What is it Lovely? Isn’t that what you want?”

“They will have him executed!” She exclaimed.

“But isn’t that what he deserves?”

“I can’t let anyone kill Abe. He’s my children’s father. Two wrongs won’t make things right. And it won’t bring my parents back or give me my eyesight,” Lovely stated.

“I think it’s too late for that Lovely. I overheard my father talking on the phone earlier, and I think he was discussing what was to be done to Abe and his crew.”

Lovely didn’t want Abe dead. She wasn’t even sure she wanted to be away from him for very long. She missed her husband; not the man that was a part of killing her parents. She longed to be in Abe’s arms and welcome that warm feeling of being safe. This was just too much for her. She let out a deep breath as she stood up.

“Where are you going?” Cesar asked.

“To take me a shower and think about some things. But first I’m calling Luciano to discuss—”

Cesar interrupted her. “No, don’t call him tonight. Let him rest. We’ll address him tomorrow. Okay?”

Lovely gave it some thought. “Okay, but first thing tomorrow. I don’t want no one else dying.”

"We'll talk about all of this tomorrow," Cesar said. "Go ahead and take your shower so you can relax for the rest of the night."

Lovely headed upstairs to his spare bedroom. Cesar waited until he heard the shower before he snuck into the bedroom. He went to the doorway of the ensuite bathroom to observe Lovely through the glass of the walk-in shower. The steam made it hard for him to see her clearly, but he could make out the silhouette of her body. Just imagining what was behind the glass aroused him. That brought a smile to his face.

Cesar backed out of the bathroom when she stopped the shower. He stood at the staircase landing which served as the entrance to the loft bedroom. He watched her as she dried herself. His eyes traveled down to her perky breasts that childbearing obviously hadn't affected. As his eyes moved further down, it pained him to see the rounded curve of her belly. She was pregnant yet again, by Abe. Anger began to manifest within Cesar and reminded him of why all of this was happening to begin with.

A continuous beep sounded.

Hearing the alert of his alarm system, snapped Cesar out of his thoughts. *What the hell? Who could have opened his door?*

Cesar cursed himself for being so foolish and not arming his security system when he and Lovely got there. Furthermore, he was upstairs when his gun was downstairs. He carefully eased down the stairs until the living room became visible; nothing.

He continued down, and out of nowhere, he was met with the force of someone's fist. He was hit hard enough that it knocked him out cold.

Hearing a thud, Lovely looked toward the staircase, "Cesar?"

She got no response, so she continued to dress in her pajamas. She called out again, "Cesar!"

Lovely went down the stairs in search of Cesar, but when she got to the bottom, she stumbled over what she assumed was his body. She gasped as she knelt down to confirm it. Frantically pushing at his lifeless body, she called out, "Cesar!"

Suddenly, she was grabbed from behind, and a hand covered her nose and mouth with a rag that held a slightly sweet smell to it. As she struggled, she slowly began to lose consciousness.

Chapter 14

Robin already had in mind what she would say to convince Lovely to go with her. She recited it over and over in her head. It sounded genuine to her. Besides, Lovely was so caring and kind she wouldn't be able to see through anything Robin had up her sleeve.

When Robin walked up to the front door of Lovely's home, she was a little irritated that the door was locked. The gate had been left open, so she assumed Lovely was back to being careless. Robin didn't understand Lovely sometimes. With everything Lovely had been through, a person would think she would always be cautious of every little move she made. Not Lovely. She just wanted to believe that all people were so damn good. Robin scoffed to herself as the thought played in her head.

She rang the doorbell and waited patiently. Seconds later, Aunt Lily answered. She greeted her with a warm smile.

"Hey, baby."

Robin returned the smile, "Hey Aunt Livy. I was just stopping by."

Aunt Livy stepped aside to allow Robin entrance. "Well, come on in. I don't understand why you won't come on back here to stay."

"Well, I like where I'm at," Robin explained as she followed Aunt Livy towards the kitchen. Something sure smelled good. Robin had to admit she missed Aunt Livy's cooking.

"You hungry?" Aunt Livy asked as she stopped in front of the pot on the stove.

"No, I'm good," Robin stated as she made her observations. There was no one in the den off from the kitchen. It was usually lively in there. "Where is everybody?"

"Let's see... Grace is with Eli and the twins. Lulu is putting the baby down in the nursery... Lovely is gone out of town," Aunt Livy answered.

Robin eyed the big pot Aunt Livy was tending to. With a confused raise of the eyebrow, she asked, "So, who are you cooking for if everybody is gone?"

"Oh chile, this is for me, and whoever else might want some," Aunt Livy chuckled. "But Abe did mention he wanted me to make him—"

"Wait, Abe? And did you say Lovely was out of town; with who?" Robin asked as she walked closer to Aunt Livy.

"Oh, she left with Cesar," Aunt Livy said nonchalantly. "You want some of this stew? You look a little frail to me. Have you been eating Robin?"

"She's out of town with Cesar?" Robin asked as she watched Aunt Livy fill a Tupperware bowl with the contents of the pot.

"She left with him earlier. You can call her on her phone. I'm sure she'll answer... well, maybe not. It's rather late, and you know Lovely is an early sleeper."

"Yeah," Robin mumbled. She removed her phone from her purse. "Well, Aunt Livy, I guess since no one is here I'll be on my merry way."

"Alright baby. You sure you don't want none of this stew?"

"I'm sure," Robin said as she headed for the foyer. She sent a text to Esau: **change of plans... lovely with cesar**

"What are you doing in my house?"

Robin's head jerked up to the sound of his voice. A menacing smile spread across her face.

"Abe? You're not supposed to be here."

"Neither are you. I put your ass out," he said.

Robin noticed the leather Givenchy duffel bag Abe was carrying. "And Lovely put you out. You must be here getting some more clothes."

"Nevermind what I'm doing," he eyed the cast her hand was in. "What happened to you?"

Robin cut her eyes at him, "You know what the fuck happened, you evil bastard."

Acting clueless, Abe said, "I have no idea what you're talking about."

"When I speak to Lovely, I'm telling her you were here," Robin taunted.

"I don't care. I'll tell her myself."

Robin scoffed with amusement. "You're an ass. And your days are numbered, you know that?"

Abe shrugged as if her words didn't faze him at all. He walked past her heading towards the kitchen. He stopped at the dining room entrance and turned to face Robin. "You know your days are numbered too, right?"

"And what does that mean?" Robin asked as she reached for the front door.

"It means you need to start telling your loved ones goodbye," he replied before giving her a wink of the eye. He turned around and walked away.

"Smug ass mothafucka," Robin said under her breath. She exited the house and headed to her car. As soon as she sat in the driver's seat her phone rang. "Hello?"

"What do you mean she's out of town with Cesar?" Esau asked with aggravation.

"I didn't know she was going anywhere!" Robin said in a higher tone than she meant to.

"This shit was supposed to happen tonight!" Esau said angrily.

"Well, you need to have a word with those other dudes. It seems like everybody got their own agendas and nobody's doing things accordingly," Robin pointed out.

Esau blew air in frustration, "Alright. You try getting a hold of her and seeing if you can plan something."

"I'll try," Robin started her engine. "Guess who I just ran into?"

"I don't care. Call Lovely!" He demanded before ending the call.

Robin rolled her eyes and sighed heavily. She immediately dialed Lovely's number but got no answer. It went straight to voicemail.

Robin thought briefly about what Abe just said. *It means you need to start telling your loved ones goodbye.* She laughed out loud. Abe had no idea.

Lovely stirred in her sleep. She fought to wake up. It felt as if she had been drugged and her lids were heavy. Her eyes fluttered open. Immediately, she sensed she wasn't in the comforts of her own home. *Where was she? What happened?*

Lovely sat up. She was in a room; on a bed, a comfortable bed. There was a light on in the room. It was dim, but it was enough for her to make out some things. Then it donned on her. She was at Cesar's place. Maybe she had been dreaming but stumbling over Cesar's body and then being grabbed from behind seemed all too real.

Lovely eased out of bed and cautiously walked to where she remembered the bedroom entrance was. Suddenly, the room didn't seem familiar at all. Nothing was where she thought it was. In fact, instead of the room having a loft effect, it felt like a closed in room. She felt along the wall until she came to what felt like a doorknob. She turned the knob only to discover that the door was to an empty closet.

Telling herself to keep calm, she continued to feel along the wall. She traced her hands along the furniture that lined the wall until she came across another doorknob. She turned this one, and she felt the resistance of a locked door. She tried again even pulling on the knob. The door was locked. She was locked inside the room.

Panic started to overcome her. She had been kidnapped! Lovely banged on the door and began shouting.

"Hey! Somebody help me!"

After screaming and carrying on like a mad woman for five minutes, Lovely realized there was no one to help her. For all she knew, she was somewhere out in the middle of nowhere. She started to cry as she thought of her children. She even thought of Abe and how he was so overprotective of her. Now she understood why.

Lovely went to one of the windows. Surprisingly, it was unlocked. She raised it open only discover that she wasn't on level ground. There was no way she was going to risk her life and her unborn babies' lives. She couldn't even determine how far up she was. So, she did the next best thing. She screamed out for help only to be answered by the familiar quiet noises of the night.

Devastation began to settle in. Feeling hopeless, Lovely climbed back into the bed and faced the door. Whoever kidnapped her would be returning. All kinds of thoughts began to play in her head. *God,* she thought, *where is Abe?*

If Abe's life was a movie, Donny Hathaway's song *Giving Up* would definitely be on the soundtrack. As he listened to the lyrics and the soulful melody, he could relate to the singer's anguish over losing his woman. The music was also very fitting for his current drunken condition. With nothing else to do, he was just sitting in his truck, listening to Donny, and drinking Louis XIII Grande Champagne Cognac. Luciano had given him the expensive vintage liquor as a celebratory gift for merging companies. Abe couldn't think of a better occasion to down the brown liquid than now; while he was having a pity party.

The aroma of the stew Aunt Livy prepared for him was invading his nostrils, but he had no appetite for it. What he really wanted to do was go on a killing spree. He would start with Esau and then end it with Cesar. Yes, Cesar had to go too. Abe didn't trust his ass, and he definitely wasn't feeling how Cesar was around Lovely. It would only be a problem down the line.

Abe's phone rang, and he looked at the display. It was the man known as his father. He answered.

"Hello?"

"Where are you, Abe? Lovely is missing!" Luciano said frantically.

"She is?" Abe asked casually. The alcohol in combination with his attitude wouldn't allow him to be worked up over what he had just heard.

"What do you mean *she is*? Yes! And we need to find her!"

"But wasn't she with Cesar?" Abe asked. "Ask that mothafucka where she at."

"Abe?"

"What?"

"Are you drunk?" Luciano asked.

"Maybe," Abe chuckled.

"Your wife is missing!" Luciano repeated loudly for emphasis.

"Well, go find her!" Abe replied.

"Where the hell are you?"

Abe looked at the house and had no clue what the address was. He replied, "Somewhere. Where Cesar's bitch ass?"

"He's right here. He said someone broke into his place, knocked him out, and took Lovely. I need you to sober up and help find your wife."

"Call the police," was Abe's reply. He suddenly had the urge to use the bathroom. "Hey, can I call you back, I gotta piss." He didn't give Luciano time to respond. He ended the call and gathered his belongings including the stew Aunt Livy made.

After wrestling with the keys, he finally was able to let himself inside the house. He headed straight for the stairs. He had to take his time because he missed a couple of steps and almost fell. His phone rang again. He didn't bother looking at it this time. He took it out of his pocket and fumbled with it until it was silenced. Not knowing what else to do with it, he tossed it over his shoulder, and it went tumbling down the stairs.

Once on the second floor, Abe walked down the hall to the bedroom at the very end. Again, he wrestled with the keys until the right one opened the door.

Abe stood in the doorway and stared at Lovely. She sat on the bed with her back pressed against the headboard. Her knees were drawn up as she hugged them. Her eyes were big and round, but instead of being bright with joy, they were filled with sadness and fear. She had been crying. This wrenched his heart with guilt and sorrow. He let the duffel bag he was carrying fall to the floor.

Lovely's voice came out small and terrified. "Please, don't hurt me. My husband will pay you whatever you want."

"I wouldn't hurt you," Abe said. "And you're right; I would pay whatever I needed to."

There was silence. Confusion etched on Lovely's face. She let go of her knees, and the sadness and fear faded from her face. It was replaced with anger and aggravation. "Abe!"

He wondered if she could see him, would she be even angrier at the silly grin he was wearing. "Baby…don't be mad."

Lovely hopped up from the bed and charged for him. "Don't be mad? You fucking kidnapped me! You sick bastard!"

Her punches only tickled him. "Will you stop? You're gonna hurt the baby."

"This isn't funny," Lovely said through gritted teeth. She hit him in the chest one last time. "I can't believe you!"

"Are you done?" Abe asked.

"Take me home! Take me home right now!" She demanded.

Abe was still holding the bag with the stew in it. He extended it to her. "I bring you a peace offering; Aunt Livy's stew."

"Fuck you!" Lovely pushed past him and walked into the dark hallway.

Abe put the food down on the nearby dresser and went after Lovely who happened to locate the staircase, "Where you going?"

"Out of here! I can't believe you did this shit!" She carefully walked down the stairs. "But then again, I can, you sicko!"

"You really don't mean that," he followed her.

"What kind of game do you think this is?" Lovely asked as she felt along the walls.

Abe walked over to the light switch and turned on the lights. “Is that better?”

“Where the fuck are we?” Lovely asked as she looked around. Nothing was familiar about where they were.

“Why are you using so much profanity?”

“Take me home!” Lovely demanded.

Abe eyed her in her pale-yellow pajama set. Her stomach was noticeably rounded. “You look really good. Yellow is your color.”

“Are you drunk?” Lovely asked.

“I think so.”

Lovely groaned with aggravation. “This is fucking great!”

“Can I just explain?” He took a careful step towards her.

“No! Take me home!”

“But you weren’t even home,” he argued.

“So! That’s where I wanna be now.”

“Okay, listen to me first,” he said as he closed in the space between them.

Lovely took a step back. “Please stay away from me Abe.”

“I can’t.”

Lovely wanted to choke the air out of his body. This was the craziest thing she could have imagined. *Who does this kind of stuff?* “Can you just take me home?”

“I love you Lovely,” he said softly.

“I’m not in the mood for this Abe; none of this. It makes no sense. You make no sense. You’re insane!”

"I know," he said. "I'm only insane without you. You are the reason for any sanity I experience. I need you Lovely."

Lovely turned away from him. "Stop it, Abe."

He reached out to touch her shoulder, but she jerked away from him. "Baby, please listen to me," he pleaded. "I never meant to hurt you. I didn't know who you were at first. I promise I didn't. And when I did know it was too late. I was in love with you... and I didn't want to lose you."

"So, kidnapping me is going to make it all better?" she asked sarcastically.

"No," he said. "I knew you would be mad about this. But... but..." he let his voice trail as he thought about Cesar. He grew angry. "I'm still your husband. And my wife ain't being around no other nigga; especially one who wanna replace me. So, fuck Cesar!"

"What are you talking about?" Lovely asked as she spun around to look at him directly.

"Cesar. He wants you. I see the way he looks at you. I see how he get all in your space. What the fuck was he doing upstairs with you?" Abe asked angrily.

"Again, what the hell are you talking about?" Lovely asked.

"When I let myself into his place, he was coming from upstairs where you were. What were y'all doing?"

"I wasn't doing anything. I had just taken a shower."

"I shoulda put a bullet in his mothafuckin head," Abe mumbled. He walked around and sat down on the sofa. "That bitch was watching you."

"What did you do to him?"

"That nigga a'ight. He living," Abe answered flippantly. "What's the history between you two?"

Lovely tensed up. "Huh?"

"Huh?" Abe mocked. He noticed Lovely becoming fidgety. "What's up with you two?"

"Nothing," she answered.

"That's okay. You don't have to tell me. I'll find out on my own," Abe said. He propped his legs up on the coffee table crossing them at the ankles.

Lovely cleared her throat uneasily. "Where are we?" she asked.

"Somewhere where we won't be bothered," he answered. Just then his phone started ringing. It was still on the floor by the staircase.

Lovely rushed over in the direction of the phone. Abe jumped up to beat her to it. She almost had her hand on it before he hurried up and snatched it up.

"What do you think you're doing?"

"Hoping to tell someone how crazy you are and that you kidnapped me."

Abe smiled down at how child-like her facial expressions were. "You're so cute."

Lovely rolled her eyes and sat down on the third to last step of the staircase. "I just wanna go home, now."

"I'll take you home... in a minute."

"Why did you kidnap me?" she asked.

"You wouldn't have walked away with me willingly, would you? I've been calling you, and you don't answer. You won't talk to me, Lovely. This was the only way."

"Why couldn't you just wait?" she asked in more cooperative tone.

"Wait for what?"

She shrugged. Abe looked at her bare dainty feet. He was compelled to touch them. She moved away from his touch. Tears welled up in his eyelids.

"I'm sorry for hurting you, Lovely."

She didn't respond. He knelt on the step before her. Despite her attempt to push him away, Abe wrapped his arms around her. "Baby, please. I can't be without you. You're my everything. Being with you has given me so much joy and peace. I can't function without you."

Lovely was such a wuss for a crying man. "Abe, stop it."

"No Lovely. Let me fix it. That's all I was trying to do. I just wanna fix it," he cried. He placed his head on her lap.

"How are you going to fix it? Can you bring my parents back, or how about my vision?" She tried to fight her own tears. "That's fixing it. Can you do any of that?"

Abe popped his head back up. "No... I can't. But can I love you?"

"That's not enough," Lovely cried.

"It's all I got."

Lovely was so confused. There was no doubt in her mind and heart that the man before her loved her. He was also the man that done one of the worst things that could have ever happened in her life. Lovely pushed Abe away from her and headed back up the stairs.

Abe just sat there, alone with his own thoughts. There was no one to blame but himself. It was his actions that got him in this predicament. And even if he killed everyone on his hit list, it wouldn't change how Lovely felt about him now. And at that moment, that's all that mattered to him.

Chapter 15

There was nothing like the soft caress of a loving, gentle touch by the person you were so deeply in love with. His touches awakened Lovely. They felt so good and reminded her of why she loved Abe so much. It wasn't the actual act of making love, but it was the fact she knew he loved her. *But how could she just overlook what he had done?*

If she pretended that she was asleep, then she wouldn't have to feel shameful for letting him touch her. However, Abe didn't stop at just caressing her. He had to remove her pajama bottoms and panties. As soon as she felt the tip of his tongue on her pussy, she accidentally let a moan escape her lips.

"Abe," she moaned as she arched her back. God, she wanted him. Her center ached, and she had to have him inside her. It didn't take long for her juices to start pouring from her love box and her legs to start trembling. As she came, he began to work his kisses up her body. He planted them all over her small mound of a belly. The feeling of his hardness gliding up her leg turned her on to the max. Her nipples were already at attention in anticipation of his tongue. He suckled them, causing them to ache even more.

Abe kissed her neck and whispered, "Are you still pretending to be sleep?"

Lovely replied, “Yeah.”

Situated in between her legs, he rose up on his haunches. Lovely let her legs fall open to welcome him in. He didn’t enter her right away. Instead, he massaged her slit from her clit to her opening with the thickness of his head. She was already sensitive, and this act alone was driving her mad crazy. But this was what Abe did. He loved teasing her, knowing she was always ready for him.

He spoke softly to her, “*Te quiero mucho mi amor. Por favor, no me dejes nunca. Usted es mi mundo.*”

Lovely responded, “*Yo también te quiero ... pero no sé si puedo perdonarte.*”

Abe entered her wetness. “Just try, Lovely.”

Lovely cried out as she received him. Her walls contracted around him the further he eased into her.

“I love you, baby,” Abe whispered as he began thrusting in and out of her in slow but deep strokes.

Why was he doing this to her? Lovely wondered. The hurt of what he had done was astounding, but his love was just that much more astonishing. He asked her not to leave him. He said she was his world. Lovely didn’t want to leave Abe. He was her husband. He was the father of Grace and AJ; not to mention the twins she was carrying. And she believed she was his world. But like she told him, she loved him, but she didn’t know if she could forgive him.

“You love me, Lovely?”

Lovely burst into tears, “Yes Abe but I don’t know...”

“Don’t cry. Baby, please don’t cry,” he said as he stopped stroking her. He sat up pulling her up into his embrace.

Lovely held onto him tightly and cried. She couldn't do it. She couldn't hate him. She probably needed to, but she just couldn't. Maybe she was confused. It was the sex. She needed to stop. They couldn't finish. But the way he was caressing her, rubbing his hands through her hair, and kissing her tenderly on the top of her head made it so hard to pull away.

Lovely lifted her head to touch his face. Once she found his lips, she kissed him wildly, deep, and passionately. She reached for his dick. It was still hard and wet from her juices. She raised up just enough to guide him inside her. With their lips still locked in a fervent kiss, Lovely began rocking her pussy back and forward on his dick. The friction it made caused her to go in a frenzy.

Lovely knew at that moment she wasn't going anywhere. She loved this man too much.

The drive home was silent except for the radio tuned into the local radio station. It gave Lovely time to reflect on the information Abe shared with her. She didn't want to hear it at first, but he made her listen. He told her everything he'd been going through trying to keep the truth from her. The blackmail, threats, and even the lies Robin told. And the kicker was when he informed Lovely that Robin had been stealing money from her all this time. Lovely really wanted to confront Robin about these things.

Abe reached over and turned the volume down on the radio.

"I know you told me nothing is going on with you and Cesar, but I don't like the way he looks at you. Are you sure there's nothing with you two?"

With reluctance, Lovely replied, "There's nothing now."

"What does that mean?"

"It means that once upon a time Cesar took an interest in me," she answered carefully.

"How long ago was this time?" Abe asked.

"Well, I was in my early twenties."

"Was it sexual?"

Lovely didn't respond. She turned toward the window on her side.

Abe asked again, this time his voice was more demanding. "Did you and Cesar fuck?"

"No," Lovely finally answered.

"But something happened," he took his free hand and took her hand in his. In a soothing tone, he said, "Talk to me, Lovely."

Lovely hesitated. "Abe, I don't really like thinking about it. It's something I've pushed way in the back of my mind. I don't even like thinking of Cesar in this way."

"Did he hurt you?" Abe asked with concern.

Lovely shook her head. "No. He didn't hurt me. I wouldn't let him. He got upset about it. We had words. He stopped talking to me for a long time, but he got over it. We decided to leave the past in the past and not bring it up again. From that point on I just looked at him as a big brother, and I was supposed to be like a little sister."

"So, he pursued you, and you shut him down?" Abe asked for clarification.

"Basically, but I think I led him on. I accepted invites to dinner and trips. We never had intercourse, but we kissed... and did other things."

"Like what?"

Lovely exhaled heavily. She said, "I let him perform orally on me."

"So this nigga know what the fuck you taste like?" Abe asked angrily.

"Abe, it was years ago," Lovely argued.

"I don't care how long ago it was," he snapped. "No wonder this nigga looking at you like he wanna eat you up."

Lovely pulled her hand away from him. "There's something else."

"What?"

She took a deep breath before speaking. "When I was fifteen I had a crush on Cesar. At that time, he was about twenty-eight. He seemed to have this obsession with me too. One night, he snuck into my bedroom. I guess he didn't want the guilt of actually having sexual intercourse with me, so he ate me out. My dad was onto him and warned him several times not to entertain the idea of ever having me. Cesar would always joke openly about how he was going to make me his wife one day. Anybody that knew my daddy knew he didn't joke around when it came to me.

"So, my daddy somehow picked the lock to my bedroom door without us realizing it. He cut on the switch and caught Cesar in between my legs. He went into a rage. I was terrified and just cried. He wanted to kill Cesar. My mother had to calm my daddy down. He let Cesar live. But what was odd about the situation was that my daddy didn't tell Luciano about it. He kept it between just the four of us: me, my mama, him, and Cesar. But a couple of weeks later, Cesar got into some accident, so we didn't see much of him around after that. I didn't see him until much later when my parents; well, you know."

Abe didn't want the conversation to lead to the incident with her parents. He felt guilty every time the subject came up. But now, he had a little more information that could answer the number one question; *why would Cesar want Dharmesh dead?* And if he was so obsessed with Lovely, *why was she ordered to be killed too?*

Later that day, when Abe and Lovely walked into their house, Luciano greeted Abe with a smack upside his head.

"*Sei fottuto pazzo! È fottuto idiota*!"

"Watch out old man," Abe chuckled as he guarded himself against another one of Luciano's smacks.

"You had us worried sick," Luciano said. He went to Lovely to examine her for any signs of distress. "Are you okay? He didn't hurt you, did he? You know I will kick his ass."

Lovely offered Luciano a small smile. "I'm okay. I just wanna see my kids," she pulled away from Luciano and headed towards the den.

Abe was about to head towards the bedroom until he saw Cesar step around the corner of the dining room. The two men locked stares. Abe noticed the bruise of his madness around Cesar's temple and eye area.

"What are you doing here?" Abe asked.

"I couldn't go out of town not knowing where Lovely was. We thought something serious happened to her," Cesar said. "Oh, and I owe you one."

"I would apologize about that, but I'm not sorry," Abe said coldly.

Luciano looked between both men with confusion. "What the hell is going on here?"

Cesar eyed Abe daring him to say anything. Abe smiled wickedly. "Cesar got something—"

"Abe," Cesar interrupted. "Can I talk to you privately?"

Abe's phone rang. He answered Cesar before he answered his phone, "No."

Luciano turned to Cesar with question. Cesar shifted his eyes from his father to Abe. If looks could kill, Cesar would have murdered Abe.

"Hello?" Abe answered his phone.

"Mama's up!" Eli screamed into the phone.

"Is she?" Abe asked.

"Yeah, get up here. She wants to see you."

"I'm on my way," Abe ended the call. He looked at Luciano, "My mama is awake."

Chapter 16

Although she was happy about Sarah awakening from her coma, Lovely opted to stay home and cuddle up with AJ. His soft coos were enough to distract her from all the craziness around her. She wished Grace was there, but she was with Eli.

Just as Lovely was placing AJ back in his crib, someone entered the nursery. Lovely looked toward them and knew who it was instantly. She didn't greet them with a smile. Flatly, she said, "Why are you here?"

"I thought we could have a girl's day out. You know, now that you're feeling better," Robin said cheerfully.

"I don't think so," Lovely stated. "As a matter of fact, I don't think I'll be going anywhere with you ever again."

Robin frowned and cocked her head to the side. "Why is that?"

"I know everything now, Robin."

"Everything?"

"Yeah, Abe told me everything."

Robin walked cautiously toward Lovely. "Abe is a liar."

"So, you were taking money from me?" Lovely asked.

Robin let out a laugh. "Is that what he told you?"

"At this point, why would Abe need to feed me a bunch of lies?"

"Because he's a compulsive liar; they don't need reasons to lie; they just do it."

"He found out about you stealing money from me, so you threatened to tell me about his involvement in my past. You know about all of that because you've been fucking Esau and his nephew, Lorenzo."

"That's a bunch of bullshit," Robin tried to dismiss.

"So, Grace is lying on you too?" Lovely asked.

"Grace? What does she know?"

"It doesn't matter. Just know that I believe Abe over you. And I'm asking you nicely to get out of my house and don't ever step foot in it again," Lovely said firmly.

"You can't be serious. You keep letting this evil mothafucka come between us."

"*Us?* I'm beginning to think the only reason you became my friend was for the perks and trying to steal money from me."

"Bitch, please," Robin scoffed. "You're mad at me, but I guess the nigga dicked you down so good it makes you overlook his shit. You act like what I did was far worse than what Abe did. Bitch, he killed your parents!"

"Get out!" Lovely ordered.

Robin stepped closer to Lovely, "Make me you blind bitch."

Lovely knew Robin would show her true colors eventually. Lovely stood her ground and didn't back down. "Do you think I'm playing?"

"I don't give a fuck if you are. My mission today is to get you to come with me and I ain't leaving this house without you."

Lovely hauled off and punched Robin in her face. Robin countered with a blow of her own. Soon, they were entangled in a brawl. The noise they made drew Lulu's attention.

"You stop it!" Lulu shouted trying to get between the two ladies. Robin managed to push her out of the way.

Thinking quickly, Robin went to AJ's crib and grabbed him up. "I swear I will throw him to the ground!"

Lovely heard AJ began to cry. She ceased all fighting. "Don't hurt my baby!"

"I won't hurt him if you do as I say," Robin said calmly.

"Okay. Robin, please," Lovely pleaded.

"It's too late for that shit," Robin spat. She looked at Lulu fumbling with her cellphone. "Put it down, Lulu!"

"I call the police!" Lulu yelled.

"Call the police, and they both will die," Robin threatened. She looked back at Lovely. "If you don't want your baby to die I suggest you follow me."

Abe was annoyed that Cesar felt a need to accompany Luciano on their way to the hospital; *why did Cesar need to tag along? Was he that afraid of Abe ratting on him?* The glances they exchanged with each other were their way of fighting in silence.

"Abe," Sarah managed to say with some excitement when he entered her hospital room.

"Mama, calm down before you flat-line," Eli said.

Sarah cut her eyes at Eli and then turned her attention back to her older son. She reached out as far as she could; causing as little pain as possible. Abe came to her and planted a kiss on her forehead.

"How are you feeling?"

"There's something I need to tell you," Sarah whispered. Just then, Luciano and Cesar walked into the room. Sarah immediately became self-conscious about her appearance. "Who told him to come up here?"

Luciano smiled and walked over to her bed. "You don't want to see me, Sarah?"

"No. I look like shit," Sarah said.

"This woman been laid up in a coma and she worried about how she look." Eli rolled his eyes in an exaggerated manner.

Luciano leaned down and pecked Sarah's cheek. "I'm glad you're okay."

Sarah straightened the nasal cannula that was looped around her ears. "You are?"

"Of course; I do care about you, Sarah," Luciano said.

"Cece ain't gon want you caring for her too much," Eli stated.

"Have the police been in here to question you about your attacker?" Abe asked.

"Yeah," Sarah nodded.

"Well, what happened?" Abe wanted to know.

Sarah glanced around the room. "I really don't remember much. It was all a blur."

"What were you doing in the projects?" Abe asked.

Sarah shrugged. "I can't remember, Abe."

"You don't remember anything, Mama?" Abe asked with impatience.

Sarah shook her head.

"What was the last thing you remember?" Abe questioned.

"Abe, you sound like the police. Stop badgering me," Sarah said.

Abe didn't like the way she was behaving. Just minutes ago, she said she needed to tell him something; now she was acting clueless. "Were you here when she was talking to the police?" He asked Eli.

"They were just leaving. Aunt Mary and Patricia were here." Eli answered. "They went down to the cafeteria."

"Who are the kids with?" Abe asked.

"I left them at the house. Grace is there. They'll be all right," Eli said nonchalantly. His eyes brightened as a thought came to him. "Hey! Did you really kidnap your wife?"

Abe grinned, "Yeah, but I told Aunt Livy."

"Abe, that wasn't funny," Luciano said.

"You kidnapped Lovely?" Sarah asked. "Why? And where is Ike?"

"Long story Mama," Abe told her.

"And Ike is across seas somewhere," Eli added.

"Across seas?" Sarah asked with confusion. "Don't he know his mama is laid up in the hospital?"

"He's on vacation," Abe said flatly.

"Vacation," Sarah said with thought. She asked Abe, "Well, what's going on with you and Lovely?" Sarah wanted to know.

"Lovely knows the truth now," Abe said.

"Even about her no good friend?" Sarah asked.

Abe and Eli shared questioning glances. Eli asked, "How do you know about Robin?"

"What about Robin?" Luciano asked.

Abe's phone rang. He answered, "Hey Lulu!"

"Abe! She took Lovely and baby!" Lulu screamed on the other end.

"What?" Abe asked with confusion.

"Robin! That bitch! She took Lovely and baby AJ!"

"Lovely left with Robin?" He asked for clarity.

"No! She took them," Lulu shouted. "She have no phone. She have no bottle for baby. She have no diaper for baby. Robin said no police or baby is dead!"

"I'll call you back, Lulu," Abe told her in haste. He looked at Sarah, "What do you know, Mama?"

Sarah was hesitant. She glanced at Cesar who was tending to his phone as he slipped out of the room. Sarah whispered, "They did this to me. I overheard them talking. They said something about kidnapping Lovely for ransom."

Luciano looked in the direction Sarah had been looking only to find that Cesar had disappeared. "Who are they, Sarah?"

Abe asked, "Are *'they'* Robin, Lorenzo, and Esau?"

Sarah looked toward her door and nodded, "Him too... and that other fellow."

"Him who?" Abe asked. He pointed toward the door, "Cesar?"

Sarah nodded.

Before Luciano could get a word in Abe bolted for the door. Eli went after him but bumped into Mary in the process.

Mary spun around in a dizzy state. She asked, "What is going on?"

"Just stay with Mama!" Eli called over his shoulder as he hurried to catch up with Abe.

Luciano ran out of the room, knocking Mary into Patricia. "Sorry ladies. Stay with Sarah!"

Cesar waited it out on the fourth-floor men's restroom. As he waited, he sent out a text: ***Come get me from Vanderbilt hospital asap!***

His phone rang. It was Luciano. He couldn't answer it. Once the calling stopped, Cesar dialed Lorenzo. As soon as

Lorenzo answered, Cesar, barked into the phone, "What's going on? Nobody said anything about taking the baby!"

"Robin said she had no choice. But the baby is just insurance, it'll guarantee that nigga's cooperation," Lorenzo explained casually.

"Look, you'll get your money, but nothing is to happen to Lovely," Cesar said.

"Well, you need to talk to your boy about that. He wanna get rid of her. She'll only be trouble down the line, Ceez."

"No, she won't. Don't touch her! I mean it." Cesar warned as a text came through.

I'm on my way

"What happened with Sarah?" Lorenzo asked.

"She didn't remember anything. I'm not worried about her. Look, let me call E to see where his head is at," Cesar hung up. His phone rang immediately. It was Esau. He anxiously answered, "Hello?"

"Are we taking her to the spot we discussed?" Esau asked.

"Yeah, and Esau... don't do anything to her or the baby. We need them in order to get the money for you guys, *capisce*?"

"Yeah, yeah, yeah... we'll wait until you get here," Esau said before ending the call.

Cesar needed all of this to play out right to work in his favor. If not, he knew he was as good as dead.

Chapter 17

Lovely held AJ close to her. He was fussy. His nap was interrupted. She could hear him suckling on his fist as a way to soothe himself. The only reason she was allowed to hold him was because Robin had to drive and there was no car seat. Lovely prayed Robin wouldn't take him from her again.

Lovely wanted to cooperate as much as possible if it would ensure the safety of her child. She dared not question Robin during the entire ride. It seemed like they had been riding on a highway for miles. Robin sang to the tunes on the radio without a care in the world. Lovely sat in the back seat, with AJ, wishing she could reach up and bang Robin's head into the steering wheel. But that would mean they would wreck.

"We're here!" Robin sang out.

The lighting went from bright to dark. Lovely assumed she either pulled into a garage, under a carport or under some shade. When Robin got out, she opened the back door for Lovely to step out.

"Come on, Lovely. We ain't got all day."

Robin's voice echoed. When Lovely eased out of the car, she immediately sensed it was in a very open space, but they were inside something like an underground parking garage. The flooring under her felt hard; like that of concrete.

Lovely asked, "Where are we?"

Robin laughed, "Like I would really tell you."

"Robin, if this is about money, we can work something out," Lovely said desperately.

"Oh, now you wanna work something out. That ain't what you were talking back at the house. You thought you were bad, didn't you?" Robin taunted.

Lovely didn't respond.

Robin pushed Lovely. "Let's go. We'll have time to chit-chat later."

Lovely tried to pay attention to the journey to their destination. They went through a heavy door, then up four flights of stairs and through another door. They traveled down a long corridor where their footsteps and AJ's cries echoed. Everything was dark, so Lovely knew there were no lights on. She knew they were in some type of building. And from the repugnant smell lingering in the air, she figured it was an abandoned building.

They turned a few corners going through two sets of double doors.

"Ah! Our guest of honor has arrived!"

Lovely cringed at the sound of his voice. From what Abe told her, it wasn't surprising to know Lorenzo was present in all of this.

"You don't have to do this. I'll give you whatever you want."

"Doing it this way is better," Lorenzo reached out and grabbed her by her arm. He told Robin, "Get the damn baby!"

"No!" Lovely cried as she tried to free herself from his grasp and hold onto AJ at the same time. The struggle caused AJ to cry again.

"Let him go, Lovely," Robin tried to peel lovely's hands from AJ.

"Please, let him stay with me!" Lovely begged as Robin tried to take AJ.

Lorenzo grabbed Lovely by her throat and spoke through clenched teeth. "Let the baby go, or I'll fuck your ass up!"

Unable to breathe and with defeat, Lovely let her hands fall from AJ. However, Lorenzo didn't loosen his grip on her neck. "Now listen! I like you, Lovely. You my baby mama and I don't wanna hurt you just yet. But if your ass don't act like you got some sense, I'll put a bullet in your mothafuckin head. All we need is one of you to get that bitch ass Abe to cooperate; you or the baby. And if I kill you, then I gotta raise our daughter on my own. You understand?"

Lovely nodded. He let her go by the neck but quickly grabbed her arm. He yanked her body in the direction he was going. He opened up a door and pushed her inside. This room was very small like a utility closet, and very dark. The door shut and Lovely cried softly. She went to the door and begged.

"Don't hurt my baby."

Lorenzo banged on the door from the other side. "Shut the fuck up!" He looked at Robin holding the crying baby. "What the fuck you gon' do with him?"

Robin tried bouncing AJ up and down to get him to be quiet. "I don't know. He needs diapers and formula."

"You didn't grab none of that shit?" Lorenzo asked angrily.

"I didn't have time," Robin answered.

"Y'all some stupid mothafuckas," Lorenzo said under his breath.

"So, what should I do?" Robin asked.

"Go get the shit!"

"What about the baby?"

"Take his crying ass with you!"

Robin hesitated, "I don't have a carseat for him. And what if someone sees me with him?"

Lorenzo blew air with annoyance. "Goddamn! Do I gotta run every mothafuckin thing!" He pulled out his phone and dialed a number. When the person answered, he said, "I need you to do me a favor... Just do what the fuck I tell you... Bitch, I owe yo' ass a beatin' any fuckin way... Now do this shit, or your punishment will be worse."

Abe was quiet. Eli didn't know if that was a good sign or if Armageddon was upon them. Eli stared at the gun Abe placed in front of him, on the table. Eli asked, "What am I supposed to do with this?"

Abe shot Eli a look that read Eli needed to shut up. Eli looked at Luciano for an answer, "Am I going with y'all?"

"No one is going with anyone right now," Luciano sat back in his chair. They were in the parlor of Luciano's mansion.

"Take the goddamn gun, Eli," Abe ordered.

"I'm shooting somebody?" Eli asked.

Luciano whispered to Eli, "Just take the gun."

"Do you even know how to shoot a gun?" Tommy, one of Luciano's henchmen asked.

"Yeah, I know how to shoot one. But it don't mean I want to," Eli looked around the room at the army of men Luciano had gathered at his home. It looked like mafia central headquarters. "So, when do we make a move?"

"They'll call," Luciano said. At that moment, Antino walked in the room.

"What's going on Lu?" Antino asked looking from Luciano to Abe.

"They got Lovely," Luciano answered.

Antino looked at Abe and tried to read him. Abe wore one of his infamous unhinged looks. He was about to explode at any minute. Antino asked, "Who has Lovely?"

"Ahkil is on his way," Luciano replied.

"Who has Lovely?" Antino repeated.

Abe answered him with the barrel of his gun pointed in Antino's face. "You got some shit to do with this?"

Antino remained calm as he responded, "No. Why would I?"

"I don't know. I'm still waiting for you to tell me why you went along with killing your brother's best friend," Abe said snidely.

Luciano stood to his feet and looked at Antino for an answer. Antino's eyes shifted to Luciano. "It's not what you think, Lu."

"Then tell me what Abe is talking about?" Luciano raised his voice. He looked around the room at the other men, and barked, "Everyone out!"

Once the others left the room, it was just Luciano, Eli, Antino, and Abe.

"He and Cesar were in on the home invasion," Abe explained. "Cesar asked Antino to hire someone to do it for him. Antino went along with it and asked me, Eric, and Lorenzo to do it. I executed it, and we took the money in the vault as payment. Of course, Antino got a cut of it."

"Pras was a fucking rat, and you know it, Lu," Antino told Luciano. "He was gonna take us all down."

"No," Luciano shook his head emphatically. "Pras would've never done that to us. I can't believe you had him killed."

"Pras sent Stefano down," Antino argued. "We were next, Lu!"

"It doesn't make sense, Antino! If we were going down, then he would have gone down with us," Luciano reasoned.

"He was making a deal with the feds. Cesar told me he was right there when Pras met up with them. So yes, when Cesar came to me about it, I had no problem with going through with the job," Antino said.

"But you were going on Cesar's word."

"Do you think your son would have lied about it?"

"I don't know what to think with all the shit going on behind my back!" Luciano exclaimed. The room fell silent, and everyone looked on while Luciano was in thought. But Abe still had the gun pointed at Antino's face. Luciano rubbed a hand over his face in a weary manner. He sighed and looked at Antino, "Where's my daughter and grandson?"

"I have no idea," Antino answered looking directly into Luciano's eyes.

Abe was ready to pull the trigger. Antino looked at Abe.

"I don't know where she is. That's my word."

Eli's phone rang. He hurried to answer it, so it wouldn't disrupt the ongoing confrontation. "Hello?"

"I just touched down," Kris said.

"That's good. Let me call you back."

"Eli!"

"What? I'm in the middle of something."

"So, you're just gonna—"

"I don't mean to cut you off, but I gotta go, Kris," Eli said.

"Okay," she managed to get out before Eli ended the call on her. Then he thought about it and called her back.

She answered, "Hello?"

"Where are you?" Eli asked.

"I'm right around the corner from your house."

"Go to David's restaurant. Tell him I sent you and you don't know what the hell is going on. He'll know what to do."

"Okay," Kris said with uncertainty.

"Kris?"

"Yeah Eli?"

"I love you." Eli ended the call.

Aisha wasn't sure what Lorenzo had going on, but he had to be out of his mind to think she was going to take care of a baby. Furthermore, she told him she was done fucking with him and his crew. She didn't want any parts of it. However, Lorenzo hadn't been so willing to let her go just like that. He had no idea she went behind his back and confided in Abe. If he ever found out she knew, he would really beat the life out of her.

Aisha drove into the dark garage parking lot of the old abandoned hospital building. *Why did he have her to meet him at this funky building with baby items?* It didn't make sense. The further she drove, she instantly recognized the black Mercedes as Robin's car. *What was she doing here?*

As instructed, Aisha went to the door straight ahead. She had to go up several flights of stairs until she came to the fourth floor. The building reeked. She was surprised that so much old equipment and furnishings stayed behind in the place.

Hearing voices and a baby crying lead her straight to where she needed to be. She looked at an angry Lorenzo and Robin, bouncing a baby in her arms.

"What the hell is going on?" Aisha asked.

"Just give her the stuff," Lorenzo ordered. "What took you so long?"

"I was just making sure I got everything you told me to get. Whose baby is this?" Aisha looked on at the fussy baby. From the amount of hair on the baby's head, it was hard for Aisha to tell if it was a boy or a girl; being that the baby was only wearing a white onesie and socks.

"Stop asking mothafuckin questions and help her with that shit," Lorenzo said, "That fuckin baby gettin' on my nerves."

Aisha looked around and could see that they were in an area that could have been a nurses' station. The space was open to two wings of the floor. Aisha placed the bags on the desk.

Robin passed the baby to Aisha. "You hold him while I fix him a bottle."

Aisha didn't know what to do with the squirming baby. She tried the bouncing thing, but the baby wasn't feeling it. The baby stopped crying long enough to focus on her face. Aisha gasped, "Is this Abe's baby?"

After Lorenzo nor Robin answered, Aisha went on, "Does he know you have his baby?"

"He knows Robin has his baby," Lorenzo said.

Aisha glared at Robin. *How could she be so evil?* Aisha felt a need to protect AJ now, so she held him close to her. "So, why does he not have any of his things? Where is the big bag that mother's carry around?"

"Will you shut up," Robin snapped. She gave Aisha the bottle. "You feed him. I have to go."

"Wait! I'm not staying here," Aisha objected.

Lorenzo looked at her. "You are now. Sit down and take care of the baby."

Aisha watched as Robin and Lorenzo disappeared around the corner where she could faintly hear other voices. *What the hell was going on?*

Lovely could hear them talking outside the door. She had been real quiet trying to use her hearing sense to its full ability. She no longer heard AJ crying in the distance. She only hoped that meant he was asleep. If they did something to her baby, Lovely wouldn't be able to live.

"C'mon Loco man. Go ahead and call that mothafucka. I'm trying to have this shit over with by tomorrow."

"Okay, okay. Damn... y'all ready?"

"Let's get this shit started."

That was Robin. Lovely thought, *If Robin was outside her door then who had AJ?*

Their voices became faint. They moved further away from her. Lovely backed away from the door and sat back in her spot on the floor. She could only imagine what was going on inside of Abe's head.

The day had gone by quickly. It was night and still no call. *What were they doing?* Abe looked at his phone for the millionth time. No missed calls. No new texts. *And where the fuck was Eric?* He spoke to him earlier, and he said he was getting Kam and the kids somewhere safe, and he would be over right after that. That was two hours ago.

"Why don't we call the police?" Eli asked.

"We don't get the police involved in shit like this. This is a matter we take into our own hands," Luciano stated.

Ahkil asked in his strong Indian accent, "And these are the same people who killed my nephew?"

Luciano glanced Abe and Antino's way. They had agreed that once Ahkil arrived that they would keep Abe and Antino's involvement in the past to themselves. He answered, "Yes, they are."

"I will kill them times two," Ahkil said. "How long have you known these were the men?"

"Just recently," Luciano answered.

"Where is Cesar?" Ahkil asked.

"I'm about to go find him in just a minute," Abe said. He didn't understand why Luciano didn't hand Cesar over to Ahkil. *Why was he protecting Cesar?* Perhaps for the same reason he was protecting Abe.

Abe's phone rang. Everyone got quiet and eagerly watched as he answered, "Hello?"

"What's up cuz," Lorenzo said casually. "Let me cut to the chase. Ain't no need in bullshitting around. You know why I'm calling. You know what it is. Check it. You give me what I ask for, and you get your wife and son back."

Abe could hear his son's cries in the background. AJ's cries alone almost broke Abe down. "What are you asking for?"

"Twenty million; once you give me the money, you get your son."

"No, you said my wife and son."

"You'll get Lovely after I've had enough time to leave. I'll call you and tell you where she is."

"How much thought did you give to this?" Abe asked.

Lorenzo chuckled, "What type of question is that? Mothafucka, I ain't stupid. So, here's the deal. My uncle will meet with you at midnight, tomorrow. You'll trade off the baby for the money."

"Tomorrow? Naw nigga, I need my wife and son back now!"

"You got twenty million in cash, on hand, now?" Lorenzo laughed, "We doing shit my way. You either cooperate, or they can die. Which way you wanna do this?"

"Fuck you," Abe hung up the phone.

"What does he want?" Ahkil asked.

Abe repeated to them everything Lorenzo said.

Luciano placed a hand on Abe's shoulder. "Son, as of right now, we cooperate and do what he asks."

Abe didn't respond. His phone rang again. It was Eric. "Where the fuck you been?"

"I took Kam and the kids to her aunt's house all the way in Smyrna. I'm on my way though."

"I just got a call from that nigga; the swap going down tomorrow. But in the meantime, I wanna try to find these niggas," Abe said.

"I'm down. Here I come."

Chapter 18

AJ was crying again. He had been fed, and his diaper had been changed. Aisha didn't know what else to do.

"Shut that baby the fuck up!" Lorenzo yelled.

"I don't know what's wrong with him," Aisha said nervously. She feared if AJ didn't get quiet Lorenzo would harm him.

Lovely's muffled voice came from the closet a few feet away. "Can I have my baby?"

"Maybe that's what's wrong with him," Aisha said. "He probably just needs his mama."

"Give him to me," Robin reached out for AJ.

Aisha gave him over. She looked at Lorenzo. "I think I need to get back home."

"You ain't going nowhere; you in this shit lil' mama," Lorenzo said.

"I won't tell anyone, Lo," Aisha said.

Lorenzo scoffed, "Yeah, like you didn't go telling Abe a bunch of shit already."

Aisha tensed up. *How did he know?* Maybe he could be just pulling her chain.

Lorenzo gave her a sinister smile. "Oh, you didn't think I knew about that? That's the reason I owe you an ass whooping."

"I didn't tell Abe anything," Aisha lied.

"You gon lie to my mu'fuckin face?" Lorenzo walked up to her.

Aisha took a step back. "I didn't tell him anything. We just talked about our lives."

"Don't fuckin play me," he jabbed her in her head with his fingers. "Bitch, I will fuck you up!"

Aisha cowered, ready to block his blows. Lucky for her, he didn't swing.

AJ was still whiny. Robin said, "Maybe Aisha is right. Let's give him to Lovely until he falls asleep."

"And where will you put him once he's sleeping?" Aisha asked.

Robin shrugged. She looked around and spotted a cardboard box. "I'll put him in there."

"That filthy box?" Aisha questioned.

"You got a better idea?" Robin asked smartly.

"Well, this isn't exactly the best place to have a baby," Aisha said. "We can barely see in here. These flashlights won't last forever."

"Will you shut the fuck up?" Lorenzo was aggravated. He gave it some thought. "Take him with you. Aisha, you stay here with me."

"I'm not staying here overnight," Aisha objected.

Lorenzo jabbed at her head again. "You do what the fuck I tell you."

Aisha had to play it cool and figure out a way to get out of this mess.

Lovely was getting tired. She tried to stay awake to listen out for AJ's cries. It gave her strength and hope. But she no longer heard him crying. In fact, she no longer heard anyone talking.

Minutes later, she heard the distinguished sound of footsteps coming towards her. The door was opened; Lovely scooted back against the wall, and a light came on.

"Can you see me, Lovely?"

Lovely tried to focus on the figure before her. The lighting wasn't enough.

"Cesar?"

"Yeah, It's me."

Lovely stood up. "You're with them?"

"I'm with myself," Cesar replied as he stood in front of her. He caressed her face with the back of his hand. "You're so beautiful Lovely?"

Lovely tried stepping back, "Why Cesar? Why are you doing this?"

"The why isn't important; just know that it needs to be done."

"But why?" Lovely's voice quivered. Cesar pressed his body into her and tried to kiss her. Lovely pushed on him, but he wouldn't budge. "Stop it, Cesar! I don't want you!"

"I love you Lovely. And when this is over with, you and I can go off and have the life people only dream of."

Was he crazy?

"I already have that life; with Abe."

"That mothafucka," Cesar said with disgust.

"What has Abe done to you that would make you do this?" Lovely asked.

"He exists. He has you. Now, he has Papa. That blue-eyed prick just got every goddamn thing. But I'm gonna get it all back."

"But you never had me, Cesar."

"Yes, I did. You were mine until your daddy came in between us."

"Is this what all of this is about? You killed my father and mother because of me? I was supposed to die too. So, you wanted me dead too, huh?"

Cesar shook his head. "No. You weren't supposed to get hurt. There was a miscommunication in the orders somewhere along the line. But baby, believe me, you were never supposed to get hurt. I was devastated when I learned of what happened to you."

Lovely started crying, "But why, Cesar? I don't understand any of this?"

"Lovely, I loved you. Your father forbade me from ever thinking of you in that way, but I couldn't help it. You know I couldn't help it. You loved me too."

"I was a young girl. I didn't know any better."

"That's not what you thought when you let me taste all of that sugar in between your legs," he rubbed her pussy through her pants for emphasis.

Lovely pushed him away from her. "You don't have a right to touch me like that."

"Abe doesn't have a right to just take what's rightfully mine. I paid the ultimate sacrifice for you. I should have ended up with you!"

"But if that's how you felt, why did you bless our marriage? You along with Luciano gave Abe your blessing to marry me."

"It was an act. I didn't think you two were really going to go through with it. My plan was to expose him a lot sooner."

"So what happened?"

"I got caught up. I got busy; y'all had that quick wedding, and it was over with."

Lovely gave it some thought as if she was having a delayed reaction. "You said sacrifice. What sacrifice are you talking about?"

Something in Cesar snapped, and his speaking became belligerent, "Your father! He did the worst thing to me that a man could suffer!"

Lovely didn't say anything. She waited for him to continue.

"You know what he did, Lovely?" Cesar was all in her face. His spittle sprinkled her. "Do you know what he did!"

"No!"

"You always ask me about not having a wife and not having children. Well, I can't have children! You father had me castrated!"

Lovely shook her head slowly in disbelief. "No Cesar."

"Yes Lovely! He did it! I gotta take hormone shots for the rest of my fucking life to feel like a man. And he had to pay for it. So, I had him killed. I had to make up a lie for my uncle to go along with it. He hired Abe. And I thought..." his voice trailed as it softened, "And I thought once your parents were out of the way, I could have you anyway... And you would love me, no matter what. But you were hurt... and I'm sorry."

"I'm sorry that happened to you. But what's this going to solve?"

"I gotta have you," he whispered in a crazed tone. He walked up on Lovely again, backing her into the shelves along the wall.

Lovely attempted to push him away, but he grabbed her arms as he tried kissing her.

"Stop Cesar! Please, stop!"

Cesar backhanded her, "You ungrateful bitch! Do you want me to let them kill you?"

Lovely was enraged. She fought back and tried to gauge his eyes out. He screamed out in pain and pushed her to the ground. She caught herself before completely hitting the floor. She grabbed for the light source which was a flashlight and swung it at him. It connected with something. She made her way to the door that he left open. Making a quick decision, she started to run to the left until she was abruptly stopped.

"Whoa! Hold up! Where do you think you're going?"

Lovely fought in the arms of whoever it was that snatched her up.

"What the fuck is going on Ceez?" Lorenzo asked. "You letting our hostage go?"

Cesar was holding his nose. "She got me with the damn flashlight."

"You let a blind bitch fuck you up?" Lorenzo joked. "Put her back in the closet, Ghost."

Lovely didn't go back in without a fight. She was screaming and punching.

Lorenzo came into the closet to assist. He punched Lovely once, and it knocked her out cold.

When Lovely came to, she had no idea what time of the day it was. Her head was hurting, and the left side of her forehead was tender. She felt woozy as she propped herself up to a sitting position. Her throat and lips were dry. They hadn't offered her anything to drink or eat since she had been there. *And where was AJ?*

Lovely stood up and went to the door. She started banging on it.

"Hey!" she called out. She did this over and over until the door was snatched open.

"Stop all that fucking noise!"

"I'm thirsty," Lovely said.

"Hey, Lo... she thirsty!" The man called out.

Lovely's head cocked to the side as she recognized his voice. "Who are you?"

He replied by shutting the door back on her. Minutes later, the door opened again. This time, it was Aisha. She handed Lovely a bottled water. She just stood there, watching Lovely as she drank the water down. Aisha had never seen Lovely so disheveled.

"Can I have more?" Lovely asked.

"I'll see," Aisha murmured as she turned away. Before closing the door, she heard Lovely heaving. She turned back to her. "You okay?"

"I think I'm going to be sick," Lovely groaned.

"Hey!" Aisha called out. "Do y'all have a trashcan or something? She gotta throw up!"

They provided a bucket just in time for Lovely to vomit all of the water she had just drunk.

"What the fuck wrong with her ass?" Lorenzo asked.

"She pregnant," Aisha said. "Can't you tell?"

"Did you know that, Ghost?" Lorenzo asked.

"Yeah, mothafucka. I been told yo' ass that," he replied.

Ghost? Lovely thought to herself; she didn't let on that she was listening.

"Aisha, go get one of those chicken sandwiches and give it to her," Lorenzo ordered.

Ghost teased, "Oh, you care about the blind, pregnant bitch."

"Fuck you. I just don't want her throwing up every goddamn where," Lorenzo said. He tapped Lovely to get her attention. “Oh, by the way, if you gotta piss or shit, use this same bucket.”

Ghost chuckled.

Aisha returned with a wrapped chicken sandwich and another bottled water. She handed them to Lovely.

Before they could close the door, Lovely asked, “Where’s my baby?”

“That lil’ blue-eyed fucka is safe,” Lorenzo told her before shutting the door.

Lovely felt around for the bucket to move it towards the corner; in doing so, she heard a vibrating sound. It did it four times before she realized the noise was coming from somewhere in the closet with her. *What the hell is that*? She thought. She didn’t hear it anymore. She sat down and began nibbling on the sandwich she was given.

Suddenly, she could hear a lot of commotion going on outside. Aisha was screaming while Lorenzo was shouting at her. The door swung open again, and there was shuffling.

Lorenzo slung Aisha’s body inside the closet. “Here bitch! You wanna do some sneaky shit. Sitcho ass in fucking time out and think about the shit you’ve done; stupid ass hoe!”

The door shut, and Aisha went to it and started jiggling the doorknob.

“Lorenzo! Let me out of here!... I wasn’t doing anything! You dumb son of a bitch!”

The door opened again, and Lorenzo snatched Aisha by her hair and punched her twice in the head. “What the fuck you call me?”

“Nothing!” Aisha cried.

"That's what the fuck I thought. Now shut the fuck up and sitcho ass down beside that hoe!"

The door shut again. Aisha cried softly as she sat down opposite of Lovely. It was pitch black, and she couldn't see a thing.

"Be careful; there're cobwebs on that side," Lovely warned.

Aisha started freaking out as she moved over to the side Lovely was on. "I can't be in here like this!"

"Where's my baby?" Lovely asked.

"Robin has him," Aisha said. There was the vibration noise. "What was that?"

"I don't know," Lovely said. "Where is Robin?"

"Somewhere, I don't know," Aisha said. "We gotta get out of here, Lovely."

"*We?* I thought you were on their side."

"You see where I'm at! I hate that mothafucka. I hope Abe kill his ass!"

"Yeah, Abe told me what you did," Lovely said.

"He told you?"

"Why did you get mixed up in all of this? Did you see it as a way to get back at Abe?"

Aisha sighed. "At first I did. But Lo is evil. All of them are."

"Where are we?" Lovely asked.

"We're at the old Nashville Memorial Hospital. It's a big building."

There was a long pause of silence. The vibration sounded off back to back four times.

Aisha whispered, "That sounds like a phone. One of them fools dropped their phone in here."

Lovely put her sandwich aside and began to feel around. Aisha joined in.

"C'mon! Vibrate again. Shit!" Aisha mumbled.

"It's over there, in the cobwebs," Lovely said.

"Get it Lovely," Aisha said.

Lovely took a deep breath and felt through the junk that was piled in the closet. The cobwebs tickled her hand, but she tried not to focus on the creepy feeling that was present. She felt around for a minute to produce nothing.

"Okay, look. We gotta get you out of here. We need to get help," Aisha said. "The next time the door open I'll ambush whoever and you make a run for it. As soon as you go out the door go to your left. Run all the way down the hall and go through the double doors. Keep going straight and go through another set of double doors. Make another left and go to the end of the hall until you can't go anymore. To the right will be a door. That's the stairwell. If you go all the way down, you will come out on the garage level. The door will be to the left."

"Why are you helping me?" Lovely asked as tears came to her eyes.

"Because it's the least I could do."

For the next thirty minutes, Lovely and Aisha tried to locate the source of the vibrating noise. Aisha was right. It was a phone. It was a standard bar style prepaid phone. Just as she was about to unlock the screen, the door swung open. Aisha quickly placed it on the lower shelf and out of view.

Lorenzo walked in and stood in front of Lovely. He looked down at her with a wicked grin.

"You finna suck my dick."

"Who?" Lovely asked.

"You," Lorenzo replied.

"Leave her alone, Lo," Aisha said.

"Bitch, you shut up!" He snapped.

"C'mon Lovely. I know you suck Abe's dick right for him," Lorenzo taunted as he rubbed himself through his pants. "Shit, I've been thinking about yo' ass for a while. You remember that night we made a baby?"

"You really are sick," Aisha said.

Lorenzo backhanded Aisha in one quick motion. "Shut the fuck up!"

Aisha whimpered in pain. The phone started vibrating. Lovely made herself go into a hysterical fit to drown out the noise of the phone. "I can't do it! I won't do it! Please... Lorenzo!"

"Shut up!" He yelled. When Lovely wouldn't quiet down, he grabbed her by the neck. "I said shut up!"

Aisha jumped up from the floor and pounced on Lorenzo's back. "Go Lovely!"

Lovely took off for the door. She could hear all of the commotions behind her as she ran as fast as she could. She made it through the first set of double doors. She pushed on, and then she heard someone quickly closing in on her. The sound of a gunshot shook her up for a moment.

"Stop running bitch!"

Another gunshot sounded off, but this one was more in the distance. As soon as Lovely made it through the second set of double doors, she was grabbed up and lifted off her feet. She tried to fight the person, but he had her arms pinned down to her side.

"Didn't I tell yo' ass!" he was out of breath. "Bitch, you gonna... make me shoot your ass."

"I just wanna go home," Lovely cried. "Please. I'll give you all of my money!"

He ignored her and carried her the entire way back to the closet. Lorenzo was going off and talking to another guy.

"Y'all bitches are working my nerves!" Lorenzo spat, "Getcho stupid ass back in here! Where the fuck you think you was gonna go? You can't see shit!"

Lovely had to catch herself to keep from falling. She stumbled over a body as the door shut again.

"Aisha?"

Lovely knelt down to feel. She shook the body but no response. "Aisha?" Lovely ran her hands along the body. It didn't take her long to figure out it was Aisha. When Lovely got to her face all she felt was a warm thick liquid. Lovely screamed out and backed away from Aisha. They killed her!

Chapter 19

The time had finally come. After spending the day preparing for what was to come, Abe was anxious to get his wife and son back home to him. Before he headed out, he made a call to Lorenzo.

"What's up, cuz," Lorenzo answered. "You got my money."

"I got it. But I need to know that Lovely and my son are okay," Abe said. He eyed Eric and Eli as they loaded up in the used car.

"They okay. You just bring that money," Lorenzo said.

"Can I at least hear Lovely's voice?"

"Hold up. You wanna hear the bitch's voice, you can hear it," Lorenzo said. Abe could hear him walking. A door opened. Lorenzo's voice boomed, "Say something!"

"Leave me alone," Lovely said. Her voice was laced with anger and sadness. Abe pinched the bridge of his nose to help hold the tears back.

"Did you hear her?" Lorenzo asked smartly.

"I heard her. I'm taking Esau the money now."

Lovely shouted in the background, "Is that Abe? Abe!"

"I promise to God, Lo, if you hurt her I will track you down and kill your ass. I promise," Abe said through gritted teeth.

"She ain't hurt. Your baby ain't either," Lorenzo ended the call.

"Fuck!" Abe yelled.

"Son," Luciano said soothingly. He rubbed Abe gently on the back. "It's gonna be alright. We'll get them back, and we'll put all of this behind us."

"And just let them go like that?" Abe asked.

"Who said we were letting them go?" Luciano said, "Oh, this motherfucker will pay for what he has done and what he is doing; one way or another."

Eric shouted from the car, "C'mon man! Time's ticking!"

Abe and Luciano shared a hug before he got in the front passenger seat. The ride was a quiet one except for Eli crunching on Cheetos in the back.

"Damn Eli! Why didn't you leave that shit at the house?" Eric asked in a teasing manner.

"Hey, I'm hungry," Eli said. "You want some?"

"Naw nigga," Eric laughed. "Now you gon' have orange fingertips!"

Abe tried to drown them out as his phone rang. He looked at the display. That was odd. *How was Eric calling him when Eric was beside him, driving?* Abe thought maybe his phone had accidentally dialed him. The ringing stopped.

Then the thought occurred to Abe that the number that showed up was a secondary phone number for Eric when he was handling *'dirty'* business. Eric mentioned he had misplaced that phone and he would have to get another one.

"Hey Eric, did you ever find your phone?" Abe asked.

"Hell naw," Eric answered. "I just went ahead and got me another one. Remind me to give you the number."

"Okay," Abe said. His phone rang again. It was funny because he saved the number under Ghost. Abe decided to answer. "Hello?"

"Oh, thank God! I finally dialed the right number!"

What the hell? Abe's heart began racing as the adrenaline rushed in. "Who is this?"

"It's me, baby. They killed Aisha, and I don't know where AJ is!"

Abe looked over at Eric who was still clowning with Eli. "I know, I know. So, why are you calling my number?" Abe hoped Lovely understood that he couldn't talk like he wanted.

"I remembered it! Abe, I can't talk for long. They don't know I have this phone. One of them dropped it."

"I understand that. But I'm kind of in the middle of something. Where are you staying again?"

"Oh. That son of a bitch must be there with you? Ghost—I mean Eric... Uhm, Aisha said I was at the old Nashville Memorial hospital building... I think the fourth—I gotta go!"

The call ended, but Abe continued to play it out. "Okay. I'll call you later. Bye."

"Who the fuck was that calling at this time of night?" Eli asked.

"Kenya," Abe lied. He cut his eyes at Eric who was acting like everything was gravy. His boy; *how could Eric turn on him like that?* Abe thought Eric would always be down with him; no matter what.

"What the fuck that bitch want?" Eric asked.

"The same shit; she wants some dick," Abe answered nonchalantly.

"You've been dicking her down, huh Abe?" Eric asked with a sly grin.

"Hell naw," Abe said, "She been asking for it though."

All kind of thoughts ran through Abe's mind. *Had Eric been against him all this time?* It didn't matter now. Abe had plans for Eric's ass too. And now that he knew where Lovely possibly was, none of them was getting out of this alive.

Abe's focus snapped back to the event that was about to take place. As agreed they were meeting Esau behind David's restaurant. Abe's plan was to hand AJ off to David and let him take him back home. They were going to let Esau take off so he would think he was getting away. However, Luciano's men Tommy and Vic were down the street, heading north. Antino's men, Carter and Travis were down the opposite end. Whichever way Esau went, they were ready to follow his ass. But there would be a change of plans.

The three men got out of the car and waited as Esau pulled up. He took his time getting out of the car with AJ. He was accompanied by two men. Abe recognized them as hanging with Lorenzo all the time.

"Give me my mothafuckin baby!" Abe demanded as he walked upon Esau. The two goons pulled out guns and pointed them at Abe. In response, Eli and Eric pointed theirs back at them.

David threw his hands in the air as he exited the back of the restaurant. "Whoa, you guys! Just do the handoff as planned. Give Abe the baby, you'll get the money. So, put the guns down before someone gets hurt."

Reluctantly they all let their guns down. Esau handed Abe the baby. It felt so good to have AJ in his arms again. Abe passed AJ off to David. David hurried back inside. Abe and Eric went to the trunk of the car and retrieved two big duffel bags. They walked over to Esau and the other two men.

"It's all there," Abe said.

The two men went to grab the duffel bags from Abe and Eric.

"It's nice doing business with you," Esau said with a smirk. "You'll get—" Esau's words were cut off by two gunshots. "What the fuck!"

The two goons tumbled to the ground.

"Abe! What the hell?" Eric questioned incredulously as he looked at the two lifeless bodies on the ground.

Eli ran over in complete confusion. "Why did you just kill them?"

"Ain't nobody surviving this," Abe said. He stared Esau down coldly. Esau didn't know what to do. He was frozen with fear.

"Abe, think about this. How are you gonna get Lovely back?" Esau said nervously as Abe walked upon him.

"I'm getting her back," Abe assured him before knocking the shit out of Esau. It made Esau stumble back onto the car. Abe began drilling his ass with punch after punch.

Eli watched in awe as his brother beat the fuck out of Esau.

Eric hollered, "Abe, that's enough!"

Abe tore away from Eric's hold and spit on Esau who was lying crumpled on the ground. "You bitch! I shoulda killed your ass a long time ago, you sorry mothafucka!"

That still wasn't enough. Abe had to stomp him twice in the head. Esau immediately went into a seizure. It didn't go on long because Abe swiftly pulled his gun out and ended Esau's life.

Abe turned to Eric and Eli. "Help me get these mothafuckas in the car."

"Abe," Eli said meekly as he went to help with one of the bodies.

"What Eli!" Abe snapped.

"You just killed my daddy," Eli said.

Abe stopped what he was doing and stood to his full height. He gave Eli a look with his head cocked to the side.

"I mean, it's no big deal," Eli said as he helped Eric toss the body in the trunk of the car. "But don't you think you overdid it?"

"Shut up Eli!" Abe said as he went on to put the other body in the trunk.

"But you did it right in front of me. A man shouldn't have to watch his father get murdered right in—" Eli stopped talking and started laughing as he ran out of the way to dodge Abe's fist. "A nigga always wanna hit on somebody. I'ma fuck you up one day!"

"Leave your brother alone," Eric said.

"Seriously Abe," Eli said as he looked at the vehicle Esau was driving. "How are you gonna follow Esau if he's dead and can't drive?"

"Follow Esau?" Eric asked. "You were gonna follow Esau?"

"That was the plan," Abe said. "Hey, let me see your gun."

Without giving it a lot of thought, Eric willingly handed Abe his gun. Eric pulled out his phone. Before he could even tap the screen, Abe shot Eric in the leg. Eric screamed out in pain.

"Aargghh! Motha-fucka! What the hell, Abe!"

Abe watched Eric hop around until he fell to the ground. "You were supposed to be my partner. Why did you turn on me?"

"What are you talking about?" Eric asked as he winced in pain.

"Your phone, your lost phone to be exact. Did you happen to lose it where Lovely is?"

"What do you mean?" Eric asked.

Abe bent down so he could look Eric in the eyes, "Your goddamn phone! That phone call I got wasn't Kenya. It was Lovely calling from your phone. She told me she's at the old Nashville Memorial Hospital building. Am I right?"

Eric started getting confused. "I don't... How... Man, you lying. Lovely can't operate a damn phone."

"You'd be surprised at what Lovely can do," Abe said.

"I don't think she blind," Eli added.

"Give me your fuckin phone! Who were you about to text, your fuck buddy, you been sucking that mothafucka's dick?" Abe snatched Eric's phone from his hand. The phone was on lock. "What's the code?"

"Abe, you tripping!"

"What's the code? I ain't gonna ask you again."

"For what! I ain't turn on you nigga!"

Abe didn't hesitate to shoot Eric in his other leg. Eric yelled out in agony.

Abe said, "I lied. I'm gonna ask you one more time. What's the fucking code to this goddamn phone?"

Breathlessly, Eric called out the code. It didn't take much searching to see that Lorenzo's and Cesar's number were both recently called numbers. Abe dialed Lorenzo and put it on speaker. He nudged Eric with his gun and told him, "Tell him Esau got the money."

Lorenzo answered, "What it do my nigga?"

"Esau got the money," Eric said.

"That's what up. He ain't being followed, or nothing is he?"

Eric looked up at Abe. Abe placed the gun up to Eric's head. Eric said, "Naw man. He should be there in a few minutes."

"Alright, bet," Lorenzo said before ending the call.

Abe and Eric stared at each other for what seemed to be an eternity. Abe finally asked, "Why?"

Eric frowned, "You ain't my mufuckin boss. I been told you that bitch needed to die. Your ass fall in love with her, and you get all fuckin soft. Besides, I needed the money."

Abe shook his head in disbelief. "I never would've thought you were so stupid, Ghost. Money nigga? I would've given you whatever you needed! You wanted the dealership. I gave you that. You wanted the club. I gave you that. Kam wanted that big ass house that y'all fucked up. Nigga, I even gave you that."

Eric chuckled, "That's just it. Cause you give a nigga something, you act like you always running shit."

"That's because I am," Abe pulled the trigger. Eric's body toppled to the ground. "Don't fuck with Fyah!"

Without being asked, Eli helped Abe get Eric's body into the car they were driving. David stood by the door with his arms folded over his chest. "Did you have to do that?"

"It had to be done," Abe said. "Ay, tell your brother to get the incinerator ready."

Lovely heard them talking outside her door. She didn't understand why they were all right there. She could only assume they were about to open the door.

"He got the money," Lorenzo said excitedly.

"This wasn't so bad after all," Robin stated cheerfully.

"I told you," Lorenzo said.

Cesar said, "Well when Esau gets here I'm gonna be on my way. Me and the misses have a flight to catch."

"The misses?" Robin asked.

"I'm taking Lovely with me," Cesar said.

"Ghost wants to kill her," Lorenzo said. He banged on the door. "You hear that? You finna die bitch!"

"No she's not," Cesar said. "It was understood that nothing is to happen to her."

"She know too much," Lorenzo argued.

"She won't tell. Trust me," Cesar said.

"Mothafucka, we don't need you no more. You can die with her!" Lorenzo threatened.

"You still need me. Don't forget, you need your new identities," Cesar said coolly.

"Fuck that shit," Lorenzo said angrily.

"Lo, calm down. He's right. We won't get far without our new identities," Robin reasoned.

The door opened. Robin and Cesar both made noises of disgust as they covered up their noses. "It smells awful in here," Robin said.

Of course, it does; Lovely thought. There was vomit and piss in a bucket along with a dead body in the middle of the floor.

Cesar reached in and grabbed Lovely by her arm.

Lovely asked, "Where am I going?"

"We're about to get out of here," Cesar answered.

"No, I'm waiting for Abe to get me," Lovely said.

"Either you stay here, and they kill you, or you come with me," Cesar said close to her ear.

"Can I just take my chances?" Lovely asked.

"Damn nigga; that bitch rather die than go with you," Lorenzo laughed. Out of nowhere, there was a loud banging on a door coming from down the hall. They all looked in that direction.

Robin whispered, "Who the hell is that?"

Lorenzo removed his gun from his back. "I don't know, but I'm about to check it out."

The banging came again. This time it was followed by a voice that boomed through the corridor. "I'm looking for Lorenzo!"

Lorenzo looked at Robin and Cesar and mouthed, "Is that Abe?"

"Lorennnnnzo!" Abe sang out.

Lorenzo drew his gun aiming it toward the end of the hall by the double doors. Cesar took this as an opportunity to start heading in the opposite direction. He pulled Lovely along, and Robin followed.

The double doors flew open. One of Lorenzo's goons who was supposed to be surveying the perimeters of the building came busting in. Without thinking, Lorenzo unloaded what was left in his gun. When he realized it wasn't Abe he had shot, he too took off in the opposite direction.

He could hear Abe's voice, "Where you going? I got your money."

Lorenzo ducked behind the nurses' station as he reloaded another clip in his gun. "Fuck you bitch!"

"I'm just trying to give you your money. A deal is a deal."

"Bring your ass nigga!" Lorenzo hollered.

Abe's wicked laugh echoed off the walls.

"Where the fuck is this nigga?" Lorenzo said to himself. *How in the hell did he find them? Did Eric play him?* Shit! Lorenzo couldn't see shit. It was too dark. He reached up to grab for one of the flashlights that was sitting on the desk. "Mothafucka, if I can't see you, I know you can't see me!"

"But I see you though," Abe said.

Lorenzo's head jerked in the direction of Abe's voice. It was no longer coming from the left. It was coming from either the right of him or directly in front of him. He sounded closer. "Fuck you! You can't see me."

"Turn that flashlight on then."

"Come out mothafucka!" Lorenzo yelled. A barrage of bullets came flying his way. One hit him in the hand knocking the gun from it. He was hit in the shoulder and in the leg. "Is that all bitch!"

A light shone on him while he sat on the floor. It wasn't Abe. It was some big Italian man, one of the guys that escorted him out at the Labor Day party.

Tommy motioned for him to get up. Lorenzo tried to feel around for his gun. Abe came from the entryway directly behind the nurses' station. He delivered a kick to Lorenzo's face that knocked him out. "I told you I saw your ass mothafucka!"

Meanwhile, Cesar was still dragging Lovely along with him down the back staircase. Robin followed right behind them. The door on the next floor opened below them. They looked at one another and decided to backtrack. Cesar led them back up to the second floor and went in through that door.

"How are we going to get out of here?" Robin whispered.

Cesar was about to answer when up ahead there were lights darting everywhere; an indication that there were people holding flashlights and searching. They couldn't go back down the staircase. He felt along the walls until he came to a doorknob. He tried it, but it didn't open.

"Hey! There's someone down there!" someone yelled.

Lovely broke away and headed back toward the staircase. Cesar called out to her, "Lovely!"

"I'll get her. She can't go far," Robin said. "I'll meet you downstairs."

Lovely guided her hands along the walls and moved as fast as she could. Robin was right behind her. Robin flashed her light and cut it off quickly just to see how far Lovely was ahead of her.

Instead of going for the staircase, Lovely took a left and went down that corridor.

Robin laughed, "Where you going?"

Lovely focused on moving ahead. She kept going until she bumped into someone head-on. She screamed.

"Lovely... Lovely, it's me!" Eli said. "I got you."

Lovely's hands were trembling as she reached up to touch Eli's face. "Eli?"

"It's me," he said.

"She's behind me!" Lovely said frantically.

"Robin?"

"Yeah..."

Eli shone his flashlight down the hall. He didn't see Robin. "I don't see her."

"She was there."

"Come on. Fuck that bitch. They'll get her ass. I need to get you to safety. You're not hurt or anything?"

"No. I just wanna leave this place," she said as she held on tight to Eli's shirt and began walking alongside him.

Out of nowhere, Robin rushed upon them. Lovely broke away from Eli's shirt. His flashlight dropped to the ground. Lovely heard Eli cry out in pain and there was a struggle. She could hear Robin growling and then there was a clank as metal met skull. It was repeated over and over and over. With each connect, Lovely could hear Eli's grunts and the breath leaving Robin's body. There was a gunshot. The struggle stopped. Then there was silence.

Lovely called out nervously, "Eli?"

"That bitch stabbed me with something," Eli groaned.

Lovely ran to his voice, "Where?"

"Shit Lovely," Eli said. "I can't die... my kids... Kris..."

"You're not going to die," Lovely said as she held onto Eli. "I bet it's just a scratch."

"Yeah, you're right. Scratches bleed like a bitch!"

Lovely felt along his body until she came to the bloody fabric of his shirt; he had been stabbed in his stomach region. Trying to remain calm and keep Eli just as calm, Lovely said, "That can be fixed."

Eli laughed. "Can it?"

"Sure. I'm a living testimony to that. If I can survive a bullet in my head, you definitely can survive this little nick," Lovely said.

Eli's laugh became weak, "If you... say... so."

"Just hold on Eli," Lovely said.

"Lovely?"

"What?"

"You stink."

Lovely laughed. "I bet I do."

Then she heard her name being called. "Lovely!"

It was Abe. She couldn't contain her excitement. "Abe! Abe! We're here!"

Eli whispered, "My brother..."

"He's coming," Lovely said. She could see flashes of lights.

"Lovely!" Abe called.

As soon as he saw her and his brother, he took off towards them.

The moment his hand touched her body, Lovely burst into tears; she felt so much relief. She felt safe again. He practically lifted her off the ground in a tight embrace.

"I love you so much. I don't know what I'd—Did they hurt you? Are you okay?" Abe asked.

Lovely nodded. "I love you too. I'm fine. But Eli's hurt."

Abe hurried to his brother's side. Eli managed to say, "Abe... you remember... when... Granny would stack all of the spam in the cabinets?"

Abe chuckled, “What?”

Lovely said, “He’s delirious.”

Eli screamed out, “I’m fucking dying!”

“No, you’re not. Shut up and save your energy,” Abe told him.

Eli whispered to Abe, “Lovely stink.”

Kris was unsure of the events that had taken place, and she was somewhat scared to even know. From the bits of information, she was able to hear in David’s home, she knew something had happened to Eli. When David told her to grab the baby and go with him, she didn’t hesitate.

Pulling up to Abe and Lovely’s home made her even more nervous. She hoped Eli was okay. She needed answers. She followed David closely as he led her through the house until they arrived in one of the main level bedrooms. She was unable to put her eyes on Eli right away due to the others surrounding the bed in the room, but she could hear him.

“Are you sure I’m not gonna die?” Eli questioned.

The white-haired man in the stark white labcoat chuckled, “I’m sure, Eli. You’re okay. It was a nice clean cut that didn’t hit anything major; lucky you. But I got you all nice and stitched and patched up. No worries.”

“Look here, Bob Barker, don’t make me have to come on down to the Price Is Right and find yo’ ass if this shit get infected,” Eli threatened.

"Will you shut up!" Abe exclaimed. "For a person that's supposed to be dying, you sure do talk a whole damn lot."

Luciano said, "I can assure you, Eli, Dr. Reische is the best. He's been making house calls for me for years."

Dr. Reische handed Eli three bottles of pills. "Here you go. Take these as needed for any discomfort, these are for inflammation, and these are to fight off the risk of infection."

Bria held up her homemade card and put it directly in Eli's face. "Look at what I made you."

"Oh," Eli said flatly. "That's nice."

Bryce snickered. "I told you it was ugly."

"How you gonna say hers is ugly?" Grace countered. "You call that mess you drew any better."

"I can draw," Bryce said. "Just like Uncle Abe. Isn't that right, Uncle Abe?"

"You sure can," Abe said.

"Y'all play nice," Aunt Livy said.

"You don't like it, Daddy?" Bria asked. A look of disappointment spread across her face.

"Of course I do," Eli said. He winced in pain as he sat up.

"Come on kids," Aunt Livy said. "Let's give your daddy some breathing room."

Bria jumped on Eli's bed to give him a hug.

Eli was hurting. "Please be careful babygirl."

"Oh, I'm sorry Daddy. I hit your boo-boo," Bria said.

"Bye Dad," Bryce said as he pecked Eli on the cheek.

"Ah, he called me Dad," Eli crooned.

"We're glad you're okay," Luciano smiled.

"Yes," Lovely said. "I don't know what I'd do without my brother."

Eli smiled, "You would miss me, Lovely?"

"Wouldn't we all?" David asked.

Eli looked at David. "When you get here?"

"I've been standing here for a minute."

"If you'd shut up for a minute, maybe your mind can focus on something else," Abe said.

"Eli?" David queried. "Aren't you forgetting about something?"

"Someone, to be exact?" Lovely added.

Eli thought about it. All of their goofy grins told him he should know what they were talking about, "Who?"

Kris appeared between Lovely and Abe. She was wearing a really pretty smile. Her hair was pinned up in a very feminine up-do. She was even wearing a dress; a black and white chevron pattern with a cropped denim jacket. Her face was lightly made up, and she wore hoop earrings.

A smile spread across Eli's lips. His eyes shifted to the baby girl she was holding.

"Hey. I forgot all about you. I'm so sorry."

"That's okay," Kris said. "I'm just glad to know you're fine. I was so worried."

"I'm still alive," Eli grinned.

Abe scoffed playfully, “That ain’t what he was saying a couple of hours ago. He was planning his whole funeral out, and the nigga just got a scratch.”

“Fuck you, Abe,” Eli shot his brother way. He looked at Kris. “Whose baby? Is that the little girl you were bringing?”

Kris looked at the baby who was about the same age as AJ. “Yes, this is Avani.”

“When you said little kid, I didn’t think you meant a baby,” Eli said.

Kris’ smile faded. “Is it a problem?”

“I mean…” Eli gave it some thought. “I guess it isn’t.”

Kris smiled again, “Good because she’s yours.”

Eli gave Kris a look. He looked at everyone else snickering, “Mine?”

“Yes,” Kris said. “This—she is what I’ve been trying to tell you about.”

Eli looked at the baby girl with her cherubic cheeks and medium brown eyes like his. She had a medium, peanut colored complexion and a lot of hair which Kris had styled with a yellow barrette in the front. He could see it.

“That’s my baby?”

“Yes!” everyone said.

“I got a baby?” Eli asked in disbelief. “When did this happen? How? Why didn’t you tell me?”

“How else are babies made?” Lovely asked.

“We’ll talk about all of that later. But do you wanna hold her?” Kris asked.

"Naw, I don't know her like that," Eli joked.

Abe rolled his eyes, "Aw hell."

EPILOGUE

Lovely remembered when she was recovering from her incident fourteen years ago, and she was wrestling with whether she should keep Grace or not. Aunt Lily told her, "*Things happen to us for a reason. Sometimes, it's just not for us to know why they just do. If you're considering keeping her accept what happened to you and move on from it for the sake of your child. Once you're okay with that, find peace with the decision you've made and look for the joy in it. She don't have to ever know how she got here. Loving her will erase the wrong that was done to you. Shoot it was only by the grace of God that both of you even survived.*"

That would always stay with her. It's what helped her get through those first few years after she had to live with her blindness. It was also those words that made it easier for her to accept Abe's role in her past. How they ended up together would remain a mystery; just something for her not to know. It was just the order of the universe.

Lovely repeated what Aunt Livy told her to Abe once she had given birth to her twins, a baby boy, and girl. She also reminded him of what he had told her when he had kidnapped her.

He said, "*Baby, please. I can't be without you. You're my everything. Being with you has given me so much joy and peace. I can't function without you.*"

That remained with her too. In fact, that whole night remained with her. But the two keywords that both Aunt Livy and Abe mentioned were *joy* and *peace*. And that's what she and Abe had with each other. She already had Grace, so Lovely thought what the hell. She named the twins Joy and Peace.

"What are you doing out here?" Abe asked snapping Lovely from her thoughts.

"Nothing," Lovely smiled. She stood on the wraparound porch, looking out into the backyard and the lake that flowed along their country getaway house. It was actually the house Abe had taken her to when he kidnapped her. Lovely had grown to love it. She loved it much better than their house in the city. They spent an amazing Christmas there with the whole family. It was very peaceful and serene. It was now Spring and the whole family was there for the Easter holiday.

Abe wrapped his arms around her from behind and held her close. He kissed her neck. "You look to be in deep thought."

Lovely held onto his arms and snuggled closer to him. "No, just reflecting."

"On what?"

"Us... life... our kids,"

"Care to share?"

"Not really. But there is something I'm curious about."

"What is that?"

"What did you do with their bodies?"

Lovely could hear Abe let out a light chuckle. “What kind of question is that?”

“C’mon Abe, I wanna know.”

“I don’t even know what you’re talking about,” he said playing innocent.

Lovely pulled away from him and turned to face him. “Stop playing.”

“Okay, okay,” he said. He looked toward the front yard and giggled. “Remember when you said you wanted the driveway to be paved out here?”

Lovely gasped, “No!”

“Ssh... Don’t tell nobody,” he said.

“Don’t tell nobody what?” Eli asked as he joined them on the porch. Kris followed behind him. She was followed by Ike and Jackie. Kris and Eli sat down side by side on the porch swing.

“About the driveway,” Abe said.

Eli grinned, “Oh, that’s that Lorenzo brand cement. And ain’t that that Esau shit on the side?”

“You’re terrible!” Lovely exclaimed. “Are you serious?”

“Yes. Now let’s not speak of it again,” Abe said.

Ike said with disappointment, “I’m still mad I missed everything.”

“You didn’t miss much,” Lovely said jokingly.

“Yeah, we were able to take care of business,” Abe said. He smiled, “You needed that vacation back then.”

Jackie rubbed Ike’s back lovingly, “We certainly did.”

Ike looked down at her and smiled, "Do you wanna go ahead and share the news?"

"What news?" Lovely asked seriously.

Blushing, Jackie said, "We're expecting."

Lovely gasped and shrieked with excitement. "I'm so happy for you two!"

"I knew it wouldn't be long," Eli said.

Kris was wearing a confused look and asked in a whisper to Eli, "Y'all got bodies buried out here for real?"

"You still stuck on that? Naw girl," Eli said. "Ain't no bodies... them mothafuckas was cremated and mixed in the cement out there."

Kris looked at Ike's, Jackie's, Lovely's, and Abe's humored expressions. "Eli, you play too much. Like I would believe some mess like that."

"You're right," Eli said. "I'm just playing." He gave Abe and Ike a knowing look that caused Abe to laugh even more.

Lovely asked Abe, "Did you send Kam that money for the kids' trust fund?"

"I did," Abe said. He felt that Kam didn't need to know the truth behind her husband's death. A part of Abe felt sad for Eric's kids, so he chose to make sure Kam and the kids were taken care of.

"You're such a good man," Lovely said as she wrapped her arms around him and placed her head on his chest.

Kris laid her head against Eli's shoulder and admired her four-carat wedding ring for the millionth time that day.

"It's so wonderful to be Mrs. Eli Masters."

"Is it?" Eli asked.

"Yes," she giggled. "He's moving," she took Eli's hand and placed it on her rounded belly. "You feel him?"

"That's him, what the hell he doing in there?" Eli asked.

Lovely pulled away from Abe and hurried over to Kris excitedly. "The baby's moving? I wanna feel?"

"Me too," Jackie said excitedly.

Peace and joy were in the air amongst their family. But there was one nagging thought that tugged at Abe every day. He looked out into the acres of greenery before him. An eerie feeling overcame him. His jaw clenched as he thought to himself, *I know you're out there... brother.*

About the Author

Ada Henderson brings her imagination to life as she writes amazing urban romance fiction under the pseudonym Ivy Symone. Writing has always been a passion of hers even before she realized that's exactly what it was: passion!

The urge to put daydreams to paper began for her at the tender age of ten. The impulse to write was sporadic over the years; but as an adult she picked writing back up, and it served as a therapeutic outlet for her. It wasn't until late 2013 that her mother encouraged her to get published.

Ivy's first debut novel was Why Should I Love You. After that, came Why Should I Love You 2 & 3, Secrets Between Her Thighs 1 & 2, Never Trust A Broken Heart, Crush 1, 2, & 3, Hate To Love You, Stay, If You're Willing, Bad Habitzz, and The Bed We Made. Ivy humbly received two AAMBC awards: 2015 Ebook of the Year and 2015 Urban Book of the Year for her phenomenal Crush series.

She currently resides in Nashville, TN with two of four children in her home. When Ivy is not reading or writing, she's enjoying cooking, watching horror movies all day long, and spending quality time with her friends and family.

CPSIA information can be obtained
at www.ICGtesting.com
Printed in the USA
LVHW081340041218
599224LV00016B/438/P